To Aunty Pam
From Marcia
+ Family

with God's richest
and the futur

SUCCESS WITHIN YOUR GRASP

Hamilton J. Williams

Dedicated to the memory of my father
Buzz Williams

Acknowledgements

Sincere appreciation to my darling wife, Julie and to my daughter Naomi who read this manuscript under an extremely tight deadline. This book reads smoother because of their comments.

To the countless others who are too numerous to mention by name, who added to my wisdom and crystallised my success principles by their willingness to allow our lives to converge. To the many brilliant authors from whom I have drawn - words are inadequate to express my indebtedness.

Cover Design by Mervyn Weir
Published by Total Health Seminars. London, England

ISBN 0-9539830-2-1

Printed in England by Century Litho Plc.
Old Print Works, Royal British Legion Industries,
Legion Village, Aylesford, Kent. ME20 7NL

TABLE OF CONTENTS

INTRODUCTION

Life is not a dress rehearsal. We only get one shot at it. Look around you. There are too many examples of people who have made a complete mess of it. It's possible even as you read this you are dissatisfied with the job you have done so far with this great gift called life. If so, that's good. It means there is awareness. Many people, battered and brutalised by life's vicissitudes are so numbed and 'spaced out' that they cannot even contemplate that there may be a better way, a higher way, a more rewarding way. They look out from eyes that have been forced to focus down in the muck and the mire. They see the world through minds that have been programmed and conditioned to fail. They believe that blind fate and circumstances favour some and curse others and that's all there is to it. For those of you who think in this vein, the material in this book is going to shock you into a glorious reality. A reality so stunning that you may be forced to say like Oprah Winfrey, "when I look into the future, it is so bright - it hurts my eyes." You have picked up the book, read on, it will change your life, it has changed mine. My only regret is that I did not get a hold of these principles when I was yet in my teens. But now that I have them, I will ride them like a horse. I will share them with all with those I come in contact with. That's what I have aimed to do in this book.

Then there are others of you. You have enjoyed some success. You have been tantalised and tickled by the fact that you can make a difference not only in your own experience, but also in the lives of your significant others. You have pushed yourself and accomplished what others thought was impossible. Yet you know that you are yet to tap into your full potential. You have won some battles and reached some goals, but you cannot verbalise or articulate the principles or the strategies that you have used. Maybe what you have done was partly by guesswork and partly by some intuition or inner conviction. As you read this book, you will recognise these principles and recognising them will enable you to use them, not haphazardly or by chance but with purpose and clarity. As a result you will win over and over again. Success is not a matter of chance. It is not a matter of the coming together of a set of favourable circumstances. Success is achieved by applying success principles. These principles will work for any one at any time and will allow you to enjoy a quality of life that you never dreamt possible.

This is not a book to read and having read, move on. This is a manual for daily living. As such I encourage you to keep it off the shelf. Keep it handy. Read a portion every day. You will find that some of the principles will jump off the page and hit you in the face only on the second or third reading. You will be amazed that the value and profundity of the principle didn't get to you before. This is because our experiences are changing everyday and the time comes when we are at the exact point when a great truth will make the greatest impact on us. We are ready for it. We will use it. We will optimise the moment. We will make a break through.

Turn the page. Say goodbye to your old limiting attitudes and habits. Begin an exciting journey into success. It's within your grasp!

Section One

A T T I T U D E

ATTITUDE

"The last of the human freedoms is the freedom to choose one's attitude in any given set of circumstances." Victor Frankl

"We build our own prisons and serve our own jailers."

"...I have set before you life and death, blessing and cursing: therefore choose life..." Deuteronomy 30:19 KJV.

The Power of Choice

**So God created man in his own image, in the image of God created he him; male and female created he them.
Genesis 1:27**

Theologians will continue to discuss and differ in their understanding of what exactly "in his own image" means. All agree however, that a significant part of this "godlikeness" is the power of choice. Human beings resemble their creator in their ability to choose. This ability to think and therefore to choose is what makes us unique creatures. Archibald MacLeish brings this thought 'in our faces' when he said, "the only thing about a man that is a man... is his mind. Everything else, you can find in a pig or a horse."[1] It seems to follow therefore that when we fail to use and develop our ability to make wise choices we are actually living our lives on the level of the brute creation. But I'm not a pig or a horse. I'm an upstanding being made in the image of God. I can think, reason, and exercise my power of choice. The more I learn to do that the more I approximate the plan God had in mind for me as the crowning act of His creation.

We must note this however: " We are free to make our choice, but after we have chosen, the choice controls us."[2] Many people stumble through life without ever coming to terms with this great principle and then are puzzled as to why they always end up at the wrong destination or in the wrong set of circumstances. I can stand on any street corner and choose to get on any bus that I want to. I have that freedom. But once I've made my choice and got on that bus, the choice now controls me - because that bus is going in a particular direction to a specific destination. I can fume and fuss all I want to, but I cannot control or redirect that bus. Of course I can exercise my power of choice to get off that bus. However, we need to note that it is not that easy to get off a moving bus. By the time I negotiate that action, I would have travelled a considerable distance off course from where I really wanted to be. So my question to you is - are you on the right bus? Did you exercise your power of choice in the direction your life is headed, or are you coasting with the tide?

Many folk believe that people are predestined for success or failure and there's nothing much anyone can do about it. But it's not the individual that is predestined; it is the 'WAY' that is predestined. Allow me to illustrate. If I go to Heathrow airport in London and board a jumbo jet flying to New York, am I predestined to end up in New York? You bet I am - once I board that jet. But am I predestined to go to New York? Of course not. I can choose to fly to any part of the world (once I have the money and my passport). But once I board that jet that is predestined to fly to New York, I am now predestined to end up in New York.

Always remember this: "we are free to make our choice but after we have chosen, the choice controls us." I've already said that haven't I? There are key thoughts and principles I will keep repeating throughout this book. I do this purposely so that there is no chance of you glossing over or missing a guiding principle. The likelihood of doing that may be greater for the speed-readers. I quite like what Jim Fiebig said: " I would rather read slowly and explore all the dungeons and secret passages than be a speed reader who bounds from parapet to parapet and thinks he has seen the castle." And that is even more relevant with the material we are dealing with in this book. I'll say things more than once in different ways and at different points until (I hope) your mind gives you the "aha" response.

As you explore this book remember at all times to **RSVP**. **R**ead, **S**tudy, **V**isualise, **P**erform. Read, read it again seeking to thoroughly understand the point. Then visualise it. See it in your mind's eye - (For some people this is more easily done by closing their eyes). Then perform some action as soon as is reasonably possible to establish the principle in your thought repertoire.

Change Your Attitude- Change Your Life!

William James of Harvard University said, "the greatest revolution of our generation is the discovery that human beings, by changing the inner attitudes of their minds, can change the outer aspects of their lives." This one idea alone is worth ten times the price you paid for this book if, you would pause and really absorb what you have just read. You can alter your life by altering your attitude of mind! Over the past months I have been experimenting with this idea in my own life and I can tell you it is awesome!

Change your attitude --change your life.

"At the core of every recurring problem there is a frozen attitude."[3]

Check it out for yourself. Your attitude is simply your settled way of thinking about a particular thing. You may think that that settled way of thinking is the only way because that's the way you have always thought about that thing. What I'm asking you to do is to challenge that settled way of thinking. Ask yourself: Is this the only way I can think about this thing? If I think of it differently, what will happen? How would I feel? How will I act? If a problem keeps recurring, you most likely have a frozen attitude. Search for that frozen attitude and work on it and you will be amazed at the results.

A young man came to me with a problem. His relatively young marriage seemed to be falling apart because of a recurring difficulty. Apart from this irritation his marriage was fine. This one area was dragging down the relationship. Here was the problem as related to me: On arriving home from work each day his wife would be very irritable. This would express itself in her finding fault with something he had done in the house, or being sarcastic in response to something he said. He on the other hand, seeing no reason for her to be like that each day, felt hurt and responded by either withdrawing or retorting in kind which only made things worse. He came hoping that I would offer some help as to what he could do about **her** problem. How could he change **her** behaviour so that things would work smoother. That attitude is a non-starter because we cannot change other people's behaviour or attitude.

I introduced the concept to him: Change your attitude - change your life. First discover your present attitude. So I asked him what was his attitude when his wife arrived home and behaved in the way he had described. He was asked to try to remember what he said to himself at those times. His answer was: "I say to myself, there she goes again. I don't deserve this. What did I do or not do this time?" I then asked him to describe how he felt when he said those things to himself. "Hurt. Sometimes a little angry. So I answer in the same mode she is in." And what's the result? "Well, it often spoils the whole evening."

I then said to him that he must try changing his attitude and see what happens. Change your attitude by saying something like this to yourself the next time your wife arrives home in an irritable mood. " I have done nothing to cause my wife to be like this, so it most likely has nothing to do with me. Maybe she has had a hard day and is tired. I will not buy into her irritability, but will be patient and wait for her to be her usual, pleasant self." I explained to him that from the time he guided his inner conversation that way, he would be able to relate to his wife differently. Guess what? The next time we met he was all smiles. The problem was solved. He said when he practised changing his attitude to be patient for the first half-hour or so after his wife arrived home from work; that was all the time she needed and she was pleasant and normal after that. We will come back to the power of monitoring one's inner conversation again.

No One Can Take It From You

"...I have learned to be content whatever the circumstances." Philippians 4:11 NIV

"Peace I leave with you; my peace I give you. I do not give to you as the world gives. Do not let your hearts be troubled and do not be afraid." John 14:27 NIV.

What is the peace "as the world gives"? That's the peace we enjoy simply because outward circumstances are favourable and peaceful. Anyone can be at peace when everything is going just right. This book is seeking to take you beyond that. To give you the tools to maintain your inner peace and equilibrium even when storms are raging on the outside. I tell you it's an awesome feeling of control of your own life when you can stay calm in the midst of a storm.

Victor Frankl, a distinguished psychiatrist and survivor of shocking cruelty at the hands of the Nazis in one of their concentration camps, says, **"the last of the human freedoms is the freedom to choose one's attitude in any given set of circumstances."** These are not mere poetic words. It was learning this that kept him free and alive in the midst of the wretchedness in a death camp.

He describes trudging through snow, ice and mud, with no socks on his feet and frost-bitten toes sticking through holes in his shoes. He recounts how the Nazis tormented him, beating him and hitting him on the back of the head with their rifle butts, and what it was like to witness friends and relatives stuffed into gas chambers or buried alive. Then, at the end of each brutal, agonising day, sick from the pangs of starvation, he and his fellow prisoners would be given a cup of watered-down soup with a single pea at the bottom of the cup as their daily ration. He tells of even having to sleep in his own excrement.

Dr. Frankl learned that by controlling his attitude, the concentration camp fell away. His mind was free to roam where he wanted it to roam, think about what he wanted it to think about; it was free as the birds - freer, really, for it could fly to the ends of the earth, to the ends of imagination, in an instant. And so can yours. But we do the opposite. We build our own prisons and serve our own jailers. But this chapter is underscoring the point that if we build the prisons ourselves, we can tear them down ourselves. You can be free of all your past limiting attitudes and behaviour!

"Attitude, being an inner thing, can keep us free-- even fairly cheerful -- regardless of the environment in which circumstances may have placed us."[4]
There is no doubt that the St. Paul had captured this winning, indomitable attitude of which we speak. No circumstance no matter how grim could conquer him. Thus he said:

"We are hard-pressed on every side, but not crushed; perplexed, but not in despair; persecuted, but not abandoned; struck down, but not destroyed." 2 Corinthians 4:8,9 NIV.

Take Charge of Your Life from Within

The average person believes that when he's caught up in a certain set of circumstances then there is only one prescribed way of reacting or thinking. Folk say things like, "what do you expect me to do under these circumstances?" Zig Ziglar says when anyone talks about being "under the circumstances" he usually asks them what are they doing under there. We let circumstances rule us, instead of realising that we can take charge and rule our lives from within. One of the most valuable things you can learn is that ultimately you're the one who's responsible for you. You don't blame others. You don't blame circumstances. You take charge.

We learn to take charge by accepting the obligations of life, by suffering, by taking risks, by loving, by bearing life's indignities with dignity. The problem with people whose attitudes do not allow for challenges and difficulties is that they have this false expectation of life. They anticipate a life without mountains to climb and chasms to negotiate. This is fooling oneself. It's not a matter of if but when. Challenges will come. Folk who don't accept this life's reality have difficulty coping when problems show up. Even Christ the great miracle-worker never promised His followers a life without hurdles and obstacles. He said very plainly in John 16:33 "...In the world you **shall** have tribulation: but be of good cheer, I have overcome the world."

"It is not what happens to you in life that makes the difference. It's how you react to each circumstance you encounter that determines the result. Every human being in the same situation has the possibilities of choosing how he will react - either positively or negatively." R.H. Schuller

"Whether life is a privilege or pain has nothing to do with the circumstances of our lives; it is a direct reflection of our attitudes. As difficult, as painful, and as unpredictable as life can be, it cannot defeat us unless we choose to be defeated."[5]

You either ride life or it rides you. Your mental attitude determines who is the rider and who is the horse.

"You don't get to choose how you're going to die, or when. You can only decide how you are going to live, now." Joan Baez

Most of us progressively narrow the scope and variety of our lives. We succeed in our field of specialisation and then become trapped in it. Nothing surprises us. We lose our sense of wonder and adventure. We do the same with our attitudes and our pattern of thinking. We so often refuse to challenge the way we think of things and accept the possibility that there may be other ways of thinking about our circumstances and handling our problems. (Or should we say our challenges?) That's an example right there. There is a big difference in viewing a difficulty as a challenge rather than a problem. Challenges tend to bring out the best in us. Problems tend to get us down.

"The things you learn in maturity seldom involve information and skills. You learn to bear the things you can't change. You learn to avoid self-pity. You learn not to burn up energy in anxiety. You learn that most people are neither for nor against you but rather are thinking about themselves. You learn that no matter how much you try to please, some people are never going to love you - a notion that troubles at first but is eventually relaxing."[6]

Though we are never free from the inevitabilities of life - illness, accidents, natural disasters, and the like - we are free to choose our attitude toward them. When the inevitabilities strike, you can choose from a number sources to inform your attitude. I choose as my unfailing guide the greatest wisdom book there is - the Bible. Here is what it tells me when life delivers an "under the belt blow." **"No temptation has seized you except what is common to man. And God is faithful; he will not let you be tempted beyond what you can bear. But when you are tempted, he will also provide a way out so that you can stand up under it."** 1 Corinthians 10:13 NIV. Wow! That's great news, isn't it? Nothing is going to happen to you today before it passes through him.

Let's look at it some more. **"No temptation has seized you except what is common to man..."** When devastating trouble comes we tell ourselves that we are most likely the only ones on the face of the earth that have to endure such harrowing circumstances. But that is not true; the trouble is 'common to man' meaning that others have had to face up to difficulties as great and greater than yours. The second thing we tell ourselves is "I can't bear this." The fact is you can and you will. The promise of the "faithful God!" is that you will not be asked to carry more than you can bear. The third thing we tell ourselves is "this time I've had it, there is absolutely no way out of this one". Wrong again. "...He will also provide a way out so that you can stand up under it."

You can choose to believe and live by the above, or hold on stubbornly to your self-defeating thinking that no other human being has had to suffer what you suffer, therefore you cannot be expected to be able to bear it and there is no way out of it in any case.

You Can Choose Your Response

"Between stimulus and response, there is a space. In that space is our power to choose our response. In our response lies our growth and our freedom."[7] Here again is another big, I mean really big and liberating concept. In simple language it is saying to us that no matter what the circumstance - even those situations in which you find yourself reacting almost instinctively in a "knee jerk" fashion - you do in fact have a space in which you can determine how you will respond to the stimulus.

So for example, when someone gives you a bad drive on the road and really "cuts you up", you do not **have** to react in the "normal" way. Between the stimulus (the bad drive) and the response (what you would normally do and say and think) there is a space in which you can **choose** how to respond. Oh, I have fun with myself and this concept. If you want to confuse people and be in control of yourself and your attitudes try implementing this concept. You will also make an interesting discovery. The more you use those "nanoseconds" the greater the space will become. The space available to you, in which you choose your response, grows as you use it.

Some of you may be saying at this point, "you don't know me. With me there is no space. I fly off the handle. I have a temper. It's in my genes." While environmental or genetic influences may be very powerful, they do not control us. We're not victims. We're not the product of our past. **We are the product of our choices.** We're response-able, able to respond, to choose beyond our moods and tendencies. We have will power to act on self-awareness, conscience and vision. "Independent will gives us power to transcend our paradigms to swim upstream, to rewrite our scripts, to act based on principle rather than reacting based on emotion or circumstance."[8] There is always hope for recovery from whatever damage our characters may have suffered due to bad genes or unfavourable circumstances. I meet people almost on a daily basis who have had some really damaging childhood experiences. These they cannot ignore and my recommendation is not that they behave as though these experiences never occurred, but neither do they need to live under the shadow for the rest of their lives. **"We are not imprisoned by our histories. There is a way out of all past damage."**[9]

Of course one must understand the difference between responding and reacting. Do you respond to the negative and make it better, or do you react to the negative and make it worse? One author said you could grasp the difference between responding and reacting if you think of visiting your doctor with a health problem and having him prescribe some medicine. On your next visit he says that your body is reacting to the medicine. That of course will cause some concern on your part, wouldn't it? But if he said, your body is responding, that will bring relief to your mind. We need to learn to respond to people's negative stimulus instead of reacting to them.

Our Lives - the result of our choices

"Our lives are the results of our choices. To blame and accuse other people, the environment, or other extrinsic factors is to choose to empower those things to control us!"[10]

On visiting a friend, one man was asked to accompany him to the corner shop to buy the morning's newspaper. When they arrived, the visitor to the area observed that his friend cheerily greeted the vendor whose response was a surly grunt. And so the visitor commented, "that man in the shop wasn't very nice, was he?" "Oh don't bother with him, he's always like that," came the reply. To which the visiting friend retorted in surprise, "always like that! Why do you bother to greet him so cheerily then?" The response was revealing. "Why should I allow him to determine my attitude?" Here was someone who had discovered the secret - that one can choose how one wanted to respond regardless of the stimulus. So many people without recognising this great truth go from day to day allowing total strangers to spoil their day. They allow other people to determine their mood and thus there blood pressure and heart rate. Now that is not very wise, is it?

Nobody is as unhappy as the person who lives his life reacting to what other people say or do. His centre of emotional gravity is not rooted within himself, where it belongs, but in the world outside him. His spiritual temperature is always being raised or lowered by the social climate around him, and so he is a mere creature at the mercy of these elements. Praise gives him a feeling of euphoria and criticism depresses him.

It is said of Christ that he was never elated by praise nor demoralised by censure. "Only a saint, of course, never reacts. But a serenity of spirit cannot be achieved until we become the masters of our own actions and attitudes, and not merely the reactors of other people's feelings. To let another determine whether we shall be rude or gracious, elated or depressed, is to relinquish control over our own personalities, which is ultimately all we possess. The only true possession is self-possession."[11]

A Way Out of All Past Damage

Having said that, there is a way out of all past damage I must emphasise here that is not to underestimate the challenge or the extent of the damage that some folk must overcome. Allow me here to touch on some areas in which many have been damaged. A recognition of this damage and a determination to climb out of the damage is what will be required if one is to soar like the eagle.

Many people have spent their entire early years surrounded by people who, with devastating inappropriateness have appointed themselves experts in the conduct of other people's lives. Sometimes these people meant well. Many times they had their own problems. But whether parents, teachers, colleagues or so-called friends, they behaved in such a way as to rob the person of every bit of self-respect or personal worth. One young lady said, "I don't remember my parents ever praising me for anything. They always had something critical to say.
When I got eight 'A' passes at 'O' level my father said it was typical that I had done well in the wrong subjects." Such a person will have a very poor self-concept, which is the person's conceptual construction of himself. He/she will be constantly seeking for outside authority to tell him/her what to do. There is a sense of worthlessness and of being doomed to rejection and disapproval.

Since "our behaviour is to a large extent an acting-out of the way we actually feel about ourselves and the world we inhabit"[12] such a person will tend to act in accordance with his evaluation of himself. He will tend to have great difficulty making decisions or in knowing what he thinks or feels.

The self-possession of which we spoke earlier will not come easily to a person who has accepted that he/she is inept, worthless and unacceptable. A process of re-education will need to be diligently pursued to re-programme what has been laid down in the subconscious mind. More will be said in coming chapters as to the importance and role of the subconscious mind in attaining success and informing attitude. But for now, to the person struggling with a distorted self-concept, the teachings of the wisdom book is crucial. You are not flotsam or jetsam on the heaving ocean of life. You were made for a purpose. You were made in the Image of God. An up-standing, intelligent being with the ability to live out the full meaning of your creation.

Dealing with People

"Hearts are flowers; they remain open to the softly falling dew, but shut up in the violent downpour of rain."[13]

"A gently answer turns away wrath, but a harsh word stirs up anger." Proverbs 15:1 NIV.

"The tongue that brings healing is a tree of life, but a deceitful tongue crushes the spirit." Proverbs 15:4 NIV.

"A patient man has great understanding, but a quick-tempered man displays folly." Proverbs 14:29 NIV.

John D. Rockefeller stated, "I will pay more for the ability to deal with people than any other ability under the sun." To cause others to want our leadership and management we must become experts in the kind of people skills to which Mr. Rockefeller was referring.

A study attributed to Harvard University found that when a person gets a job, 85% of the time it is because of their attitude, and only 15% of the time because of how smart they are or how many facts and figures they know. Surprisingly, almost 100% of education money goes to teach facts and figures which account for only 15% of success in work![14]

"Ability without the right attitude is wasted."[15] I've met a lot of brilliant people. Brilliant in terms of academic prowess and yet they never really get ahead in life because they have not learned the skills of getting along with others. People with a negative attitude have a hard time keeping friendships, jobs, marriages and relationships. Instead of exercising the discipline of working on their attitude many go through life changing jobs or marriage partners. It is easier, more rewarding and far less stressful changing one's attitude rather than one's job or marriage partner. The strange thing is that intelligent as some of these people are they hold to the idea that the problem is with others rather than themselves. If things keep going wrong with your relationships and you are in constant conflict with those around you common sense should dictate that you examine your attitude.

"When you master the Human Relations Habit, it leads to a triple win: You make others feel better; you feel better; and, directly or indirectly, your goodwill toward others will come back to you with interest somewhere down the life road."[16]

The hardest way to impress people is to **try** to impress people. You have to merit respect and let it come naturally. The least amount of respect and praise comes your way when you seek it the most. A person gets into trouble when he starts trying to be someone other than who he really is.[17]

"Other people will react to you the way you tell them to. What you do, how you act, the way you dress or the way you introduce yourself tells other people how to treat you. They will in almost every case, go along with you."[18] It's amazing how naïve people can be in this area. They dress in a particular way and when people relate to them based on the message they're sending by their dress they become upset and cannot understand why people consistently treat them in this way.

"There's no worse blow to our relation with others than to display arrogance in victory.[19] So you've won the argument or maybe you were the top salesperson in your company for the past six months or your proposal was accepted above the others -- so what do you do? Strut around the office? Flaunt the success in the faces of others? They will hate your guts for it. What a difference it will make in terms of your relationships if you demonstrate humility in your victory.

Jean Paul Richter said, " A man takes contradiction and advice much more easily than people think, only he will not bear it when violently given, even if it is well-founded. Hearts are flowers; they remain open to the softly falling dew, but shut up in the violent downpour of rain."[20]

Nothing can be more devastating than public censure. All instructive or critical feedback must be given in private. Praise must be done in public.[21]

People don't care how much you know, until they know how much you care ... about them.[22]

Tolerance is one of the most difficult human relations habits to master, because it requires looking past our own beliefs and perceptions and respecting another's right to embrace different beliefs and perceptions.

Manipulation is getting people to act for you in ways that may not necessarily be for their own good. Motivation is helping people recognise mutual interests and getting them to join the "cause," because there is a benefit for them as well as you.[23] Manipulation may get a lot of things done - for a time. But its success - if we can call it that - is short-lived. If you are a manipulator, sometime soon you will find yourself a very lonely and sad person.

Loud threats often indicate deep fears.

Making a habit of being compassionate costs nothing but is worth everything.

Attitude in Communication

"Many of the qualities and actions that lead to superior human relations are inextricably tied to effective communication."[24] Therefore any effort made to become a more effective communicator will be more than worth the effort. It is so, because no matter what your status in life; no matter what your gifts and life work may be, human relations feature in some form to a greater or lesser degree. And we're dealing with attitude here. The first attitude to this is to treat it as important. How you communicate with people is important. The benefits will be more than worth the effort you make to communicate effectively, compassionately and clearly.

One of the greatest inhibitors to effective communication is the simple word assume.

Our assumption leads to our attitudes, which leads to our behaviour. Communication can be very difficult and it takes constant concise effort to make sure you're understood. For instance, the five hundred most commonly used words in the English language have about fourteen thousand different meanings.[25] It is not uncommon to hear people say, "you misunderstood me," or "you misunderstood what I meant." They believe that it's the other person's problem for misunderstanding what they said or meant. Absolutely not. It is the responsibility of the communicator to ensure that he/she is understood.

If I treat everyone as if they're hurting, I will be treating most of them right. Pastor Bill Weber says: You can go up to anyone on the street and say to them, I heard about your problem, and they will reply, who told you? A sensitivity to the needs of others will make us more effective in leadership roles.[26]

Ralph Ringer puts it slightly different he says, "The average person is in pain, and if you don't take that factor into consideration before speaking or acting, you can neither help others nor can you gain their co-operation."[27]

When others deal with us in a dogmatic or even in a mean and vicious way, it doesn't necessarily mean they want to hurt us. It could mean, and generally does, that they are acting that way because they're hurting. If you will remember that every obnoxious act is a cry for help, you are way ahead of the game. Recognising and accepting this fact makes it easier for us to take a calmer, more level-headed approach to our functions as leaders of people.[29]

Our Attitude to Criticism

"When someone criticises you, remember, their criticism is probably an expression of their own insecurity and doubt, or of their own anger which is not necessarily directed at you. You just happen to be there at the time."[30] From the time you begin to think in this way it gives you the leverage you need to take charge of the situation and not get sucked into a reacting mode. If you get caught in reacting to that criticism, then you are allowing that person to get the upper hand, disturb your equilibrium; possibly sour your mood, raise your blood pressure and inform how you feel about yourself. That's way too much power over your life to hand over to someone.

A second way of looking at criticism is to remember that "whenever people succeed in life, petty people will take cracks at them and try to pull them down."[31] To get involved in any altercation with them over the criticism levelled at you is simply to climb down to the petty level at which they're operating. No. Stay with the big ideas, the big dreams, the gracious attitude and the uplifting thoughts. Don't become haughty either. I always check the criticism to see if there is anything I can learn from it. I usually can.

What Shiv says can make you even feel that you're not doing so well if you're not criticised. He said, "The tree that bears the most fruits also gets the most stones…unjust criticism really is a compliment in disguise. Average people hate winners. When people are not successful, critics have nothing to talk about."[32] No one throws stones at a dead dog.

To laugh is to risk appearing the fool.
To weep is to risk appearing sentimental.
To reach for another is to risk involvement.
To expose your feelings is to risk exposing your true self.
To place your ideas, your dreams, before a crowd is to risk their loss.
To love is to risk not being loved in return.
To live is to risk dying.
To believe is to risk despair.
To try is to risk failure.
But risks must be taken, because the greatest hazard in life is to risk nothing.

The people who risk nothing, do nothing, have nothing, are nothing.
They may avoid suffering and sorrow, but they cannot learn, feel, change, grow and love.
Chained by their attitudes they are slaves; they have forfeited their freedom.
Only a person who risks is free.

Sometimes we feel so hurt by criticism because we think too highly of ourselves. When I'm tempted to allow criticism to get to me too deeply this is the way my inner conversation goes: "Who do you think you are that you should not be criticised? The Perfect One, Jesus Christ Himself was criticised and ridiculed to the point of being spat upon and finally crucified. And He was perfect." That kind of inner talk usually puts things in perspective in a hurry and I often end up laughing at myself for being so taken aback by criticism. Everyone needs to feel appreciated. But anyone who thinks he or she is indispensable should stick a finger into a bowl of water and notice the hole it leaves when it's pulled out.

Then again I must realise that everyone who takes up this book to read will have some negative traits and habits. Maybe you recognise in your self the tendency to put people down. Please remember that "to push people down, you have to go down with them."[33] Try it. You can never remain standing tall while pushing someone down. You also must go down. And the lower you want to push them is the lower you must stoop. "Enlarging others makes you larger."[34]

"There is no better catalyst for getting results than gaining the goodwill of others."[35] How do we do that? Here are a few pointers:
Practice generosity it is a sign of emotional maturity.
Tact is the ability to make a point without alienating the other person.
Courtesy is an offshoot of deep moral behaviour. It costs nothing but pays well.
Rudeness is the weak person's imitation of strength.

"When someone blushes with embarrassment, when someone carries away an ache, when something sacred is made to appear common, when someone's weakness provides the laughter, when profanity is required to make it funny, when a child is brought to tears or when everyone can't join in the laughter, it's a poor joke."
-Cliff Thomas

So You Want to Change Your Attitude?

Good for you. "Change is the law of life. And those who look only to the past or the present are sure to miss the future." John F. Kennedy

"Everything is constantly changing and yet most people refuse to accept that premise in one crucial area of their lives -- their attitudes about themselves and their abilities… 'that's the way I am' is one of the most negatively powerful sentences in the English language."[36] If that's the way you are means that you're not prepared to put in some hard work and discipline to change your attitude, let's hope you're happy with your life as it is and the results you're getting. Accept the fact - no change in your attitude means no change in your life. In fact, there most likely will be change, but not in the direction you had hoped. Negative attitudes unattended may bring more negative results than in the past.

But if you do want to change that's the **first big step**. I mean recognising that you can benefit with a change of attitude. That's the hardest step. Usually people with the worse attitude problem believe that it's the other people around them who have the problem. Take a big hint if you're are constantly in conflict with people - at home, in the office, with friends, neighbours, other road users. All those people can't be the problem and you the o.k. one. The chances are even if you're not having people problems in all those areas, your life, your career, your relationships can receive a big boost with an attitude overhaul.

The **second step** is to become aware of the principles that build a positive attitude.

Most of our attitudes are shaped during our formative years. The wisdom book says, **"Train up a child in the way he should go: and when he is old, he will not depart from it.** Proverbs 22:6 KJV. The primary factors that determine our attitude are: environment, experience and education.

Nurture and develop those traits that build a positive attitude. People with positive attitudes are caring, confident, patient, and humble. They have high expectations of themselves and others. They anticipate positive outcomes. Most people find what they are looking for.

The **third step** is to desire to be positive. Desire acts as the fuel, the energy to get anything done. Many people know what's lacking in their lives. They have a good idea what needs to be done, but they lack the desire to get moving. Without the desire, ten years from now you will be in the exact spot you're today. Desire or motivation is so important that we will dedicate some more time to it later in this book. Jesus Christ always checked people's desire even before he performed a miracle. He asked some very obvious and what some may consider unnecessary questions at times. Of the man who had been crippled for 38 years lying in a wasted condition by the pool of Bethesda, Jesus asked: "Do you want to get well?" John 5:6 NIV. Now what kind of question is that? Sick for 38 years and you're asking me **if** I want to get well? But Jesus was not only checking, but also awakening the desire, for without desire nothing much will happen.

The **fourth step** is to cultivate the discipline and dedication to practice those principles. Stop procrastinating. If it's worth doing - it's worth doing now. The answer is now and we are here. Practice the positive attitude habits. Practice until it becomes a habit. It's not a matter of your feelings and your pride. If you need to go to that person and smooth the waters even if he was the wrong party, then do it. No one said it was easy. Jesus wasn't guessing when he said if someone has ought against you, you go to him and make things right. Matthew 5:23

Dr. William Glasser, the distinguished psychiatrist and author of Reality Therapy and Schools Without Failure says, " If you want to change attitudes, start with a change in behaviour." In other words begin to act the part, as well as you can, of the person you would rather be. Gradually the old person will fade away.[37]

"...whatever you ask for in prayer, believe that you have received it, and it will be yours." Mark 11:24 Notice, the wisdom book does not say believe that you will receive it, rather believe you have received it. In the words of William Glasser "begin to act the part."

The **fifth step** is to become aware of your inner conversation or self-talk. **It is your inner conversation-** what you keep saying to yourself- **that determines your attitude.** The most profound positive change that can take place in your life in regards to your attitude will happen when you begin to hear what you're saying to yourself. I'll make this point more than once in this book. This is not a passing point. It is not something to say, "oh yes, that's true" and then move on. We'll talk some more about the significance of one's inner conversation when we discuss the subconscious mind. But for now, please note that you talk to yourself constantly. Right at this moment as you read - you're talking to yourself and telling yourself something about what you're reading. That something you're telling yourself is determining your attitude to what you're reading. You're either saying something along the lines of -"this is great stuff, I believe this information can really change my life and help me to take control of my life." Or you're saying " he's making too much of a deal of this thing, it's o.k. information but I don't really believe that it will make all the difference he's claiming." And what you're saying to yourself about the information you're reading is informing your attitude towards the information and will therefore determine how much you get out of this material.

The important point to note is that unless you begin to practice catching yourself out much of your inner conversation will not come across to you as just something you're saying to yourself and therefore can be challenged. Much of it comes to mind as powerful, unquestionable rules of life. For example you may be late for work one morning and as you're about to rush out you say to yourself -"I must never leave home with my bed unmade." Well, says who? It may be a good habit to make one's bed before leaving the house each day but it's hardly a place for one of those "I must never" statements. That may be simply something you're repeating to yourself that you've picked up in childhood or wherever. You may want to hold to the habit, but challenge it and maybe change the message you give to yourself to more accurately reflect the importance of the activity. "It is a good practice to make my bed before leaving home each day" is a more wholesome message to give oneself for something as mundane as making one's bed.

Someone answers you abruptly in answer to a question at your work place. What you tell yourself - the inner conversation that takes place - will determine your attitude towards that person and can colour the relationship for a long time. You can say, "he/she is so uncouth. If that's the way he/she wants to play it then two can play the game. From now on I'll be just as curt."

You have just informed your attitude towards that person in a way that will not bring joy or satisfaction to you in the long run. Why not try changing your inner conversation to something like " um that was pretty abrupt, maybe he/she is tired or upset about something. I'll try again later." All you have changed is your inner conversation but with that change, you will feel better inwardly and pave the way for continued good relationships with that person. Indeed it's highly possible that the individual was going through a bad patch at that moment. You will be glad that you didn't react and you will feel more in control of your life and emotions.

References -

[1]Nightingale, Earl (1993) **The Essence of Success** p. 444 Nightingale-Conant Corporation Niles, Oregon.

[2]Khera, Shiv (1998) **You Can Win** p. 42 Simon & Schuster Pte Ltd, Singapore

[3]Nixon, Richard (1973) **The Lazy Man's Way To Riches** p. 172 F.P Publishing Co. Inc.

[4]Nightingale, Earl (1993) **The Essence of Success** p. 360 Nightingale-Conant Corporation, Niles, Oregon.

[5]McNally, David (1990) **Even Eagles Need a Push** p. 147 Dell Publishing New York, N.Y.

[6]Nightingale, Earl (1993) **The Essence of Success** p. 318

[7]Covey, R. Stephen, Merrill, A. Roger, Merrill, R. Rebecca (1994) **First Things First** p. 59 Simon & Schuster New York

[8]Ibid.

[9]Hart, Dr. D. Archibald (1996) **Habits of the Mind** p. 29 Word Publishing USA

[10]Covey, R. Stephen (1994) **First Things First** p. 70

[11]Nightingale, Earl (1993) **The Essence of Success** p. 263

[12]Mearns, Dave & Thorne, Brian (1988) p. 6 Sage Publications Ltd. London

[13]Zizlar, Zig (1986) **Top Performance** p. 60 The Berkley Publishing Group, New York

[14]Khera, Shiv (1998) **You Can Win** p.3

[15]Ibid. p.18

[16]Ringer, Robert (1990) **The Ten Habits of Highly Successful People** p. 114 Advantage Quest Publications, Malaysia

[17]Ibid. p.122

[18]Nixon, Richard (1973) **The Lazy Man's Way To Riches** p. 177

[19]Ringer, Robert (1990) **The Ten Habits of Highly Successful People** p.125

[20]Zizlar, Zig (1986) **Top Performance** p.60

[21]Ibid. p.62

[22]Zizlar, Zig (1986) **Top Performance** p.110

[23]Ibid. p.198

[24]Ringer, Robert (1990) **The Ten Habits of Highly Successful People** p.114

[25]Zizlar, Zig (1986) **Top Performance** p.120

[26]Ibid. p.178

[27]Ringer, Robert (1990) **The Ten Habits of Highly Successful People** p.116

[28]Ibid.

[29]Zizlar, Zig (1986) **Top Performance** p.22

[30]Nixon, Richard (1973) **The Lazy Man's Way To Riches** p.141

[31]Khera, Shiv (1998) **You Can Win** p.27

[32]Ibid. p.138

[33]Maxwell, John C. (1998) **The 21 Irrefutable LAWS OF LEADERSHIP** P.131 Thomas Nelson Inc. Nashville, Tennessee

[34]Ibid.

[35]Ringer, Robert (1990) **The Ten Habits of Highly Successful People** p.139

[36]Nixon, Richard (1973) **The Lazy Man's Way To Riches** p.107

[37]Nightingale, Earl (1993) **The Essence of Success** p.361

Section Two

MANAGING YOUR INNER WORLD

MANAGING YOUR INNER WORLD

As a man thinks in his heart (mind) so is he.
Proverbs 23:7

A man is what he thinks about all day long.
Ralph Waldo Emerson

We become what we habitually think about.
Earl Nightingale

The ability to reason, to choose, to think is the greatest gift given to us. "... And it is here we find the greatest paradox: With this greatest gift of all, the great majority of people neither know they have it, or use it... Each of them have been given the greatest gift on earth and they won't even open the box."[1]

Universities have proven that most of us are operating on about 10 percent or less of our abilities. Ten percent! And most of us think we have been stretching ourselves when we've not even begun to tap into the vast resources that the Creator has placed at our disposal.

"Your brain is no stronger than your weakest thought, and your character no more virtuous than your most private reflections."[2]

Take Charge of Your Thoughts

"Keep thy heart (mind) **with all diligence; for out of it are the issues of life."** Proverbs 4:23

"The illiterate individual of the future will not be the person who does not know how to read, but the person who does not know how to think."[3]

A healthy mind has more to do with habits than with intelligence.[4]
"Thoughts are the essential ingredients for living, and they underlie all our actions and feelings." If we want to improve our circumstances and emotions, we must first be willing to improve our thoughts."[5] The average person has not come to the realisation that he can control his thoughts. People generally allow thoughts to run riot in their minds - any subject, any time, without the slightest notion that it does not have to be so. Here again is the great news- you can take charge. In fact, you better take charge of your thoughts if you want to take charge of your life! "Take charge of your thoughts. You can do what you will with them." Plato

"...whatever is true, whatever is noble, whatever is right, whatever is pure, whatever is lovely, whatever is admirable- if anything is excellent or praiseworthy-think about such things." Philippians 4:8 NIV.

"Your thoughts create your reality and your thoughts will create your future. Change your thoughts and you change your life..."[6] Do you get the feeling that I'm repeating myself? Have I run out of things to say? I have not. I'm repeating myself purposely because it's not that easy for this message to sink in: You can change the way you think![7] You've got to accept the responsibility for your thoughts. "Bad thinking can destroy our lives just as cancer can destroy our bodies."[8]

Every person's mind is his kingdom. And he as the reigning monarch decides what kind of a kingdom it is to be; bleak or bountiful, rich or poor, interesting or dull, happy or unhappy.9 And the most important moment of our lives is when we understand that we can fashion our minds as we will.10 There is something free, liberating, exciting, and self-esteem-boosting in this wonderful knowledge. Grab a hold of it. Don't let this fact lie dormant. Use it! Exploit it! Explore it! "We can fashion our minds as we will." Wow!

In John Milton's Paradise Lost, Satan says, "The mind is its own place and in itself can make a heaven of hell, a hell of heaven." When Satan says this, he does not realise its truth or the ironic fact that his hate-filled mind has indeed made for him "a hell of heaven," but cannot make a "heaven of hell."11 We all know people who have that ability. They can take the most sublime moment and cheapen it to dung. They can be in the midst of the most unforgettable experience and by an inept comment spoil it for everybody else - unless those other people have learnt how to block out poisonous thoughts or attitudes.

When various diseases attack our bodies, our immune system fights back to keep us healthy. Most people are in the same way affected by "mental viruses" or what I call "poisonous thoughts" and we need to fight them with an injection of wholesome thoughts.

Avoid Pre-cooked Ideas

"Test everything. Hold on to the good." 1Thessalonians 5:21 NIV.

"Then we will no longer be infants, tossed back and forth by the waves, and blown here and there by every wind of teaching and by the cunning and craftiness of men in their deceitful scheming." Ephesians 4:14 NIV.

We are imposing on our minds the same burdens we have inflicted on our stomachs-- pre-cooked ideas."[12] Learn to think. Practice challenging foregone conclusions to see if they can stand up to the light of intelligent investigation. The first time you attempt to really think it will hurt your head, you'll actually get a headache, but persevere and it will become a habit. Soon, like a muscle that is exercised becomes strong, your thinking processes will become strong and vibrant and you too will be numbered among the thinkers of this generation.

"Central to critical thinking is the capacity to imagine and explore alternatives to existing ways of thinking and living.... Critical thinkers are continually exploring new ways of thinking about aspects of their lives."[13] Maintain an expansive mental paradigm. " If you wait until you're desperate before considering unconventional or extreme alternatives, that's probably how you'll live the remainder of your life - desperate."[14]

Intellect or Emotion?

"I applied my heart to what I observed and learned a lesson from what I saw." Proverbs 24:32 NIV

"The fact is that most people live in a totally unreal world. Rather than loving truth, people try to make true that which they love."[15] I see this everyday. People are not really interested in discovering the truth about life and living. They have already made up their minds and they will do anything and go to any lengths to find evidence (if one can call it evidence) to support the conclusions they have already reached.

Even if something is quite obvious to others, "human beings have a tendency to wave aside the obvious. Intellectually, we may agree with a point that's apparent, but when the time comes to act, we often ignore our intellect and act on emotion."[16] You won't believe the important decisions we make based not on fact, but on emotion - our feelings. I'm talking about big stuff: a life companion, buying a house, buying a car. I'm not saying that one's emotions should not be involved. Of course emotion is an integral part of the transaction, but if the decision is based on one's emotion, trouble is brewing up ahead. There is no clearer way to observe this than in some young couples "falling in love" and wanting to get married, waving aside the obvious incompatibility and sometimes other disturbing faults of the one on whom the love is bestowed.

The delayed response to any serious question is the first sign of intelligence -- the first sign of thought. By the delayed response you protect yourself from the damaging effects of conclusion jumping. **"Ponder the path of thy feet, and let all thy ways be established."** Proverbs 4:26 KJV.

"If you want to change your mind, you have to change what you tell yourself is true."
"Your thoughts create your reality and your thoughts will create your future - Change your thoughts and you change your life..."[17]

The subconscious mind

"It is our less conscious thoughts and our less conscious actions which mainly mould our lives and the lives of those who spring from us." Samuel Butler
When a thought or belief is conscious we can control it. We know it's there. We can examine it, challenge it, throw it out if needs be. But when that same thought or belief is buried in the subconscious, it informs our moods, our daily actions and rules our lives, without us being the wiser as to why we feel so strongly on a particular subject or why - without any logical reason - we live our lives in a certain way.

The subconscious levels of the mind, while powerful are non-critical. What is fed into it is accepted as fact without any regard to logic or later learning... The fears and repressed impressions of your childhood years, based on the most childish lack of understanding, often rule your activities today."18
Allow me to illustrate how what is recorded or accepted in the subconscious can profoundly affect our lives even when it may be contrary to present understanding.
A mother was being extremely hard on her children for placing their hats on their beds at any time even for a moment. Her reaction went beyond being tidy, for as I said, even if it was just for a moment, she would react very strongly. The children found it puzzling and upsetting because - as they said - her reaction was out of proportion with the misdemeanour. When

asked why she reacted so strongly and why it was such an unchangeable rule that hats must not be placed on the bed, the mother herself could not come up with a reasonable answer. All she knew was that one should not place hats on beds.

It was only much later the reason came out in counselling. When this mother was a child, there was a problem at one time with head lice in the school that she attended. As a precaution, to avoid the problem coming into their home, her mother had made a very strong rule that as children they were not, under any circumstances, to place their hats on the bed on returning from school. Of course this was a logical, reasonable precaution for the situation back then. Now as a mother herself she acted out the message that was in her subconscious and accepted as a general rule of life that one must not place hats on beds. Even though she had forgotten the incident with the school's lice problem, the ruling had remained in her subconscious and influenced her present habits even though the reason behind the ruling no longer applied.

The power of the subconscious is dramatically demonstrated in cases of hypnotism. In hypnotism the hypnotist bypasses the conscious mind with its reasoning ability and gives a message directly to the subconscious mind. On awakening, the conscious mind is unaware of the message, but with the right cue the subconscious mind compels the person to carry out the action, regardless of whether it's an action that will be condoned by the person's conscious mind or not. We marvel at that without realising that we send messages to our subconscious mind all day long and then we wonder why we feel compelled to do certain things, or why we find it well nigh impossible to break certain habits. It is because we keep "hypnotising" ourselves by giving messages to the subconscious. The hypnotist has perfected the art of doing this. We hit upon the principle by chance. We do it haphazardly, without even realising what or when we're doing it.

"The subconscious has no sense of humour and it accepts everything as deadly serious, even when you say things in fun."[19] So for example, you say in jest (hopefully) "I'm such a fool." You say that often enough and it records in your subconscious as fact. Your subconscious mind cannot take a joke. Another big point to underscore is this: Are you ready for this? When once your subconscious mind accepts something as fact, it will "move heaven and earth" to carry out that thing, to make it reality. Have you heard of self-fulfilling prophecy? Have you been puzzled over the fact that the very thing people fear most seems to happen to them? It therefore becomes extremely important and crucial to know how we use our minds and imagination.

When a person repeats a belief for long enough, it sinks into the subconscious and becomes reality. Auto-suggestion is a repetitive process through which we feed our subconscious with positive statements which translate into reality. Repetition alone is not enough, unless it is accompanied by visualisation i.e. feelings and emotions.

Auto-suggestions should not be practised in a negative way e.g. I am not going to fail. Positive statements should be used because we think in pictures and not in words. If I say, "Don't think of the red-faced monkey," what is the first picture that comes to your mind? The red-faced monkey.

Keep in mind too that the brain cannot tell the difference between a real experience and an imagined one. If you begin to think of a past embarrassing situation, your brain will not be able to tell that it is not the *actual* situation and therefore your body will begin to respond exactly as if you were in the actual situation.

Anything you can do without thinking is because the skill is now laid down in the subconscious mind. Like riding a bike or driving a car. One has to exert considerable conscious effort and practice until the activity becomes a habit, meaning it is now well established within the subconscious. Now this is very useful for certain activities. It's great when riding a bicycle, not to have to be concentrating on keeping one's balance all the time. Riding would be a real chore if one had to do that. The act of driving a car is laid down in the subconscious. This can be dangerous at times, like when you have covered a considerable number of miles, arrive at your destination and can't remember passing any of the places through which you have driven. Your conscious mind was engaged elsewhere, while your subconscious mind was driving the car. That's neat you may think. But if the police had a way of determining that, they would charge you for driving without due care and attention!

Just as you may drive your car every day mostly without conscious thought, so it is possible to make decisions out of habit. "...most people fail to realise that a lot of small decisions, which are usually made without thinking, are more important than the few major ones that they really think of as life-changing decisions."[20]

"He who does anything because it is the custom, makes no choice." John Stuart Mill

Most of us make virtually all our decisions, important or unimportant, out of habit. And those few that are not made automatically, the thought processes that go into our decision making are dominated by our attitudes which are just habits of thought about ourselves, our abilities and our environment. And most of our attitudes are not valid most of the time."[21]

"...the changing of your life is the creation of **conscious access to the computer of your subconscious mind!** Make no mistake, ordinary people never learn to use the great Subconscious Computer. The day they learn to use it, they cease to be ordinary."[22]
You begin by becoming aware that there is this awesome computer ticking away and controlling your life. If you are not aware of it's existence then it has full sway. Even becoming aware of it is only the very first step in taking control. You become aware by examining your thoughts, your attitudes and your beliefs. Ask yourself, why do I feel this way? Is it valid? Why do I feel so strongly on this minor matter? Why do I find it impossible to let it go? You then begin to become self-aware. When you make the subconscious conscious, then you begin to take control.

"The subconscious mind, has a tremendous power over you. It can make you wealthy or keep you in poverty."[23]

Self-talk or Inner Conversation

What ever you say to yourself determines your feelings and behaviour.

"Healthy and successful people are able to recognise and stop their negative self-talk."[24] Many people do not even realise that they carry on a running conversation with themselves. Some even believe that it's only mentally unstable people that talk to themselves. I say the opposite: If you *don't* talk to yourself then you're in serious trouble. We all talk to ourselves. Unfortunately much of it is negative. But you can change that!

Increase the awareness of what you say to yourself. Many years of irrational self-talk are difficult to eradicate. But be patient and persistent. The rewards will be more than worth the effort. Here is a big tip. "Repeat to yourself, as often as possible, a new thought to replace the old. Slowly you will come to believe it. Repetition in self-talk will change your thoughts."[25]

Fortunately, the subconscious does only what it is told. Fortunately, you are in control of this mighty power because you, the conscious you, can totally control the instructions the subconscious receives."[26]

"By keeping ourselves alert to what is going on in our minds and by being curious and observant about our thinking, we can avoid the blind spots that characterise unhealthy and unsuccessful people."[27]

For example, saying to yourself, " *I can't stand it! The noise is driving me crazy*" doesn't remove the irritation; it merely prescribes how you are going to feel. The truth is that you can stand it, and it will not drive you crazy. Learn to speak the truth to yourself. Find an alternative that will realistically address the problem.[28]

Here's another example. You have just awoken from sleep. It's 6 a.m. You look out your window and it's a dark, cold, rainy winter's morning. What do you say to yourself? Maybe you say? "*It's a nasty morning.*" You have just informed your body how to respond and how to feel maybe for the rest of the day. Try this. In a situation like the one described above, consciously change the negative self-talk. Say something like this to yourself and see what happens: " *Wow, it's raining and it's cold but it's so great to be alive! I have a full day ahead of me. A day full of opportunities and challenges. I am ready to meet today.*" I'll guarantee that your day will be different.

Focus on this one: Someone has just executed an atrocious driving manoeuvre that necessitated you applying sudden brakes. What do you say to yourself? How do you react? What you say to yourself determines how you react. If you say, "*You stupid incompetent, moron - you deserve to be punished,*" you will most likely find your blood pressure rising and your hand glued to the horn button. But if you say to yourself (and you can try this next time) "*That wasn't a nice piece of driving, but I've done worse in my time; I hope you reach on time for that important appointment you seem to be hurrying to.*" I guarantee that you will not only be able to keep your hand off the horn button, but your blood pressure will stay normal and a smile will come over your face, because you will feel good that you didn't allow a complete stranger to control a little part of your life.

What You Say About Yourself to Yourself

"An inadequate self-image is the giant controller of your personal destiny."[29]
"You may not believe what others tell you, but you always believe what your inner voice tells you, even if it puts you down - especially if it puts you down."[30] "True belief in your ability

to attain your purpose and the fundamental goals that support your purpose will grow in direct proportion to your level of positive self-esteem and even to your self-images."[31]

It doesn't help to be harsh and critical with yourself. If you have made a mistake or done something foolish, instead of berating yourself or attempting to punish yourself, ask "What can I learn from this experience that will help me to be a better or more efficient person?" That approach will not only be healthier but more helpful as well. When I begin to get angry with myself for some mistake or action, I stop the negative and self-defeating talk and say to myself, if you're so upset about it then take the necessary action so that it does not happen again. So now drop it. I actually say that to myself. "Now drop it. The issue is closed." You've got to take yourself in hand.

"A man can stand a lot as long as he can stand himself. He can live without hope, without friends, without books, even without music, as long as he can listen to his own thoughts." Axel Munthe. In fact one of the hallmarks of mental maturity and emotional intelligence is the ability to be quiet with oneself. Some folk can't stand their own company. They cannot be alone without being lonely or depressed. If they're alone they must have some noise going - the radio, the television, or something stuck in their ears going boom, boom, boom. If you can't stand some solitude without becoming restless then you need to take a hold of the way you think and what's happening in your life.

"When we are unable to find tranquillity within ourselves, it is useless to seek it elsewhere." La Rochefoucacauld **"Great peace have they which love thy law: and nothing shall offend them."** Psalm 119:165 KJV.

"No one can produce great things who is not thoroughly sincere in dealing with himself."[32]

Many men who think they have arrived are surprised to learn that they have been travelling in reverse gear.

"Worries are almost always expressed in the mind's ear, not its eye - that is, in words, not images - a fact that has significance for controlling worry."[33]

When you constantly worry about every conceivable disaster that could occur, you're practising in your imagination - practising failure, therefore guaranteeing that the thing you're most afraid of will happen, because what you practice and think about mentally, you will do.

"Your mind is an incredible success machine. Whatever you programme it to do, it will accomplish. Mentally rehearse and practice success and your mind will figure out a way for you to do it."[34]

Visualisation

People who were able to visualise what they wanted, have accomplished phenomenal achievements. I dare say you will not find a single athlete who has made it to the top who has not learned the principle of visualisation. Everyone of them before that race or event **saw** themselves winning and not only winning, but also saw themselves climbing the blocks to accept the gold. I am yet to meet or hear of an athlete who was unable to do that and yet won. You've got to learn to visualise the goals that you want to accomplish - to see it in vivid colour, to taste it, feel it, smell it. It's only then you know it's within your grasp.

If you can't see it then you're almost sure it will elude you.

Maxwell puts it this way: "If you can't confidently make the trip in your mind, you're not going to be able to take it in real life."[35] Another of my favourite authors puts it poetically when he said: "The mind attracts the physical representation of that which it holds as an image. It works by subconsciously guiding you into the correct actions to bring about the manifestation of your vision."[36]

And on and on, great authors who have discovered this very principle through travelling from different points, say it in their own way and own style and I trust that the way one of them says it hits the nail on the head for you.

"Anything you ardently desire, sincerely believe in, vividly imagine and enthusiastically act upon, must inevitably come to pass." *Paul Meyer*

Pay rapt attention here. You have just read a statement that will revolutionise your entire life if you truly absorb it. Please read it again slowly and understand what you're reading.

On checking carefully you will most likely discover that any worthwhile goal you have ever achieved; any outstanding accomplishment you have attained; any physical, emotional or spiritual mountain you have scaled; it was because you passed through this route. You ardently desired it, you sincerely believed in it, vividly imagined it and enthusiastically acted upon it. Think back on your outstanding achievements and you will verify my statement. Of course you never thought it through this way. You therefore landed on this tremendous success secret by chance or you have used it haphazardly. You have used it before and it has worked wonders for you. Now I'm asking you to use it consciously and purposefully and new power and success will flood your life in an almost frightening way.

Ardently Desire It - Do you really want it? If you do, you are in business. If not, forget it and move on to something you really desire. When I talk about 'desire' in this context I want you to think about going for days without water or food - at those points you 'desire' food and water. (Some of you won't need to go days to experience this.) What are the features of desire in this context? The hunger, the thirst is constantly with you. It is not something you forget and come back to some time later. It's there with you every moment of your life. It nags at you, gnaws at you, demands that you do something about it. It will not leave you. The intensity does not diminish with the passing of time. It will wake you up in the middle of the night - excite you, trouble you, nudge you, until you say ok, Ok, OK! I'll do something about it. That's what we mean by 'ardently desiring'.

Even Jesus Christ the great miracle worker seemed not to be able to perform his miracles without this ingredient in the recipient of the miracle. Once he met a man who was an invalid for 38 years sitting by a pool called Bethesda in ancient Jerusalem. He walks up to the man and what does he ask? "*Do you want to get well?*" Now what kind of question is that? If I were to walk into a hospital and asked someone who has been in pain for 38 years if he wanted to get well, most likely the person would be outraged by the question. Thirty-eight years of sitting like a shadow of a human being in a public place and being treated like trash and you're asking me - do I want to get well? But Jesus asked it anyway. What was he doing? He was checking the level of the desire. It is significant that the man, rather than answer the question posed, began to make excuses why he was in the condition he was in. Jesus however, sensed what he was looking for and said to the man, "Get up! Pick up your mat and walk." John 5:8 NIV. Regardless of the reasons that got you where you are today, if the desire is there you can get up from your crippling, limiting condition. You too can walk!

Again the Master Teacher met a man who was a blind beggar. This time Jesus did two strange things. Firstly, he said to the people around - "call him." Not "bring him" or "lead him to me" but "call him." The easiest thing was for Jesus to go over to the blind man. But he did not. "Call him," he said. Bartimaeus had to *show desire*. He had to get up and stumble in his blindness to Christ. Now standing before the greatest miracle-worker of all times, Bartimaeus had to answer a question with an "oh so obvious" answer: "*what do you want me to do for you?*" What was Jesus doing? Checking on, drawing out the desire. The blind man said, "*Rabbi, I want to see.*" Mark 10:51 NIV. Think for a moment the depth of feeling and desire that was in that statement and that's what we mean when we say to ardently desire something.

Sincerely Believe It

You can't really fool yourself. Except you have lost touch with reality and your mental faculty has become compromised, you know at some level if you really believe something or not. You've got to do your homework on yourself and determine whether you believe in the journey upon which you have embarked. It's a waste of valuable time and emotional, physical and financial resources to begin something when you do not believe in it with your whole being. It's extremely unlikely that you would be able to drum up the determination; sustain the momentum, generate the enthusiasm or negotiate the obstacles to carry a project to completion if there is the least doubt in your mind about its validity or meaning to you.

It is this quality of belief based on homework done that caused St. Paul to exclaim, " I know whom I have believed, and am convinced that he is able to guard what I have entrusted to him…" 2 Timothy 1:12 NIV. Again one feels the power of belief coming through in the mind of this intellectual genius of the Christian faith when he said: "For I am convinced that neither death nor life, neither angels nor demons, neither the present nor the future, nor any powers, neither height nor depth, nor anything else in all creation, will be able to separate us from the love of God that is in Christ Jesus our Lord." Romans 8:38,39 NIV. Ask yourself - *do I believe it?* If the answer is yes, beyond the shadow of a doubt yes, then an amazing power will attend your efforts.

Sincerely believing something is not only a time for your reality check, but even more so an opportunity for you to check your motives. A big and crucial question is why do you want what you want? You may ardently desire as much as you want, vividly imagine it, enthusiastically act upon it but if at the core of the entire transaction there is a selfish motive then you're working against success principles and more so against universal laws. You may even achieve some "success" but it will not last and you will not be happy or fulfilled. So selfish motives are roadblocks to the success you seek. **"When you ask, you do not receive, because you ask with wrong motives, that you may spend what you get on your pleasures."** James 4:3 NIV. The King James puts it even stronger it says, "...that you may consume it upon your lusts." That puts it into perspective, doesn't it? To sincerely believe is to check that your motives are pure. If not work on it, before you proceed

Vividly Imagine It - "There is a direct correlation between what the mind visualises and the results a person achieves." Dr Karl Pribram - neurosurgeon - Stanford University.
"You might say that a good way to start getting what you want is to develop the habit of imagining that you already have it."37 The Gospel writer Mark records Jesus as saying: **"Therefore I tell you, whatever you ask for in prayer, believe that you have received it, and it will be yours."** Mark 11:24 NIV. If you don't truly believe something you will have problems visualising it. If you're having problems holding strong mental images of that goal you want to accomplish, then back up and go back to the "sincerely believing" part of this procedure.

When asked how he accounted for his amazing inventive genius, Thomas Alva Edison replied, "It is because I never think in words; I think in pictures." Edison was told no light could exist in a vacuum, but he visualised it and believed it could be done.

The experts scoffed at Louis Pasteur's theories of germ life. Willam Harvey's far-out notion that blood flowed through the body was rejected, and Samuel Langley's vision for a flying machine was ridiculed; however, each of these men were able to visualise their dream into reality.[38] Conrad Hilton said, "Man, with God's help and personal dedication, is capable of anything he can dream." Visualise your dreams! The Bible puts it this way: **I can do all things through Christ who strengthens me.** Phillipians 4:13 KJV.

Enthusiastically Act Upon It - If you think that all what we have been talking about is some magic potion of positive thinking, then this should bring you back to reality. Ardent desire, sincere belief and vivid imagining are no substitutes for enthusiastic, robust, dogged, educated action. Read the chapter that's coming up on determination and catch the vision of what it takes to succeed beyond the ordinary.

A person without enthusiasm is like a car without gasoline. And that's what this entire book is all about, teaching you how to motivate yourself. Read and re-read and learn the lessons well and then world look - out we've got a person who will not be stopped!

Don't use your mind for garbage

I've referred to toxic or poisonous thoughts before. There are some emotions that will drain you of life-giving energy and actually undermine your immune system. One such is the hunger for revenge. "When the tongue of malice and slander, the persecution of inferiority tempt you to retaliate, when for an instant you forget yourself so far as to hunger for revenge, be calm. ... No person in the world ever attempted to wrong another without being injured in return some way, somehow, sometime."[39] **Remain calm.** A classic example of this exemplary inner calm and control was at the trial of Jesus Christ. Mark reports: **"And the chief priests accused him of many things: but he answered nothing. And Pilate asked him again, saying, answerest thou nothing? Behold how many things they witness against thee. But Jesus yet answered nothing; so that Pilate marvelled."** Mark 15:3-5 KJV.

"It is the unfailing mark of the little person - the person who has failed to grow - to spend his life dreaming and plotting to "get even" for real or fancied injuries. History shows that a person who wants revenge brings it only upon himself."[40]

"It is hard to fight an enemy who has outposts in your head."[41]

Abraham Lincoln was famous for not holding grudges. He placed his political enemies, Stanton, Seward and Chase, into his presidential cabinet.

Emotional roadblocks are among our worst enemies: Envy, jealousy, greed, revenge, bitterness, resentment, hatred, prejudice and guilt. Harbour these in your mind and you're courting failure in your life. Be merciless in your effort to root out these thoughts and emotions out of your mind. Once again: You cannot win. You will not succeed if the above list of roadblocks sit in your mind. Discipline yourself until you are able to move on from these toxic emotions. Here is what this great wisdom book, the Bible says about some of these toxic emotions.

"A sound heart (mind) **is the life of the flesh: but envy the rottenness of the bones."** Proverbs 14:30 KJV.

"...jealousy is cruel as the grave..." Solomon's Song 8:6 KJV.

"A greedy man brings trouble to his family..." Proverbs 15:27 NIV.

"Let all bitterness, and wrath, and anger, and clamour, and evil speaking, be put away from you, with all malice..." Ephesians 4:31 KJV.

The safest and best way to punish one who has done you an injustice is to do him a kind deed in return.

When someone says, "they say so and so" ask him/her to name who "they" are and watch him squirm with embarrassment.

"Nothing vivifies, and nothing kills like the emotions." Joseph Roux. So use your emotional powers don't allow them to enslave you. Your emotional reactions are simply a product of your attitudes and your attitudes can be changed, if you really want to change them.

What Is Mental Health?

Jahoda (1958) developed a list of six criteria for positive mental health.

1. A positive attitude towards oneself - self-acceptance.
2. A continual growth or movement toward self-actualisation.
3. A sense of purpose or meaning in one's life.
4. The ability to function independently or autonomously in the world.
5. The ability to perceive reality without significant distortion.
6. The attainment of mastery in the environment i.e. adequate in love and competent in work.

Richard Kinnier also has his criteria that he puts into nine categories and I include them here for comparison and also so that you can take note of the elements that appear in both lists.

1. Self-love but not self-infatuation.
2. Self-knowledge.
3. Self-confidence.
4. A clear though slightly optimistic perception of reality.
5. Courage and resilience.
6. Balance and moderation.
7. Love of others.
8. Love of life.
9. Purpose of life.

I could not help but notice that the Christian who follows closely the teachings of Jesus Christ, is in a much better position to meet these criteria. The process of leading a person to fully accept Christ and begin living as he outlined greatly assists in the fulfilment of the above list. To say it another way, accepting Christ as one's Lord and hero, so to speak, and faithfully seeking to follow his way of life from day to day leads not only to spiritual growth and maturity but also to psychological or mental health. Allow me to elaborate.

Self-love but not Self-Infatuation

When one accepts Christ as his standard, hero or pattern and views oneself through the eyes of one's Saviour one sees two pictures. One sees the inestimable value placed on one's life. Accepting the biblical teaching that Christ left the glories of heaven to die not just 'for the world of lost sinners' but for me as an individual. Christ would have done it had I been the only sinner on earth. When this first dawns upon the mind of the individual, it takes some doing to believe it at first. Then comes an incredulous wonderment that 'I am of value, inestimable value! I am somebody. I am now a child of the heavenly King!'

This invariably puts a spring in the step, a raising of the drooping shoulders, a raising of the head. Seeing one's self through the eyes of the 'Saviour' helps one to see the potential - not only the despicable character one may be presently, but also what one can become in Christ. This does not lead to self-infatuation because the other picture is there to balance things out. The closer one gets to Christ and his perfect life, the more all the deformities of ones character are revealed. One is not blinded to the shortcomings, but the love of Christ gives hope and prevents despair at what is seen. The person who lives close to Christ knows himself. His own 'righteousness is like filthy rags' but that does not depress him, for he also knows that he can find forgiveness, pardon and have his imperfections taken care of by what Christ is willing to do for him.

Perception of Reality without Significant Distortion

A clear though slightly optimistic perception of reality is how Kinnier puts it. When one becomes a Christian, reality comes into focus (or should do). The frills, the dressing, the masks are stripped away and one is faced with the fact of what life is really about. This can be shocking to some, who for a life-time have been using different crutches rather than facing up to the reality. The reality hits us when we understand that the bible settles the nature/nurture debate for us when the Psalmist David said that we were "born in sin and shaped in iniquity" - when we realise that our condition is like "an unclean thing, from head to toe we are filled with putrefying sores and there is no soundness in us." However, because of what Christ offers, the shock of facing up to reality without distorting in order to survive mentally becomes attainable.

What is it that this Jesus Christ offers that helps the individual to be able to face up to reality? He offers:

Knowledge -- "Learn of me, for I am meek and lowly in heart and you will find rest unto your souls." Matthew 11:29 KJV.

Constant Companionship -- "I will never leave you nor forsake you." Hebrews 13:5 KJV.

Forgiveness -- "Come now and let us reason together… though your sins be as scarlet they shall be as white as snow…" Isaiah 1:18 KJV.

Hope -- "Which hope we have as an anchor of the soul..." Hebrews 6:19 KJV.

Powerful Assistance -- "I can do all things through Christ who strengthens me." Philippians 4:13 KJV.

For every crushing reality that can bring despair Christ offers the answer. So although the reality may be grim, the Christian can still face up to it optimistically. To me, the realities of our modern day world are so alarming, that no amount of counselling skill that is devoid of the promises, power and presence of a Saviour like Christ can ever be adequate. We are not to underestimate the devastating effect nor trivialise the problems people bring to us, neither are we to despair with them. We can help them and ourselves see clearly and realistically what and how serious the problems are and then lead them into the help that Christ offers.

Balance and Moderation

Kinnier's balance and moderation could be taken directly out of our concept of how life would be lived in the experience of the person who has given his life to Christ. We recognise it under the caption of Temperance - the moderate use of that which is good and the total abstinence from that which is bad or harmful. This principle ought to pervade each and every part of life. Many problems, psychological and otherwise, can be traced to the breaking or ignoring of this principle. As a result of excesses, imbalance is experienced and the person loses touch with reality or the ability to cope with the challenges of life. The religion of Christ teaches temperance in all things. Adequate rest and sleep, daily physical exercise, balanced nutrition, a sensible balancing of the time spent between work and the family, spiritual endeavour and seeing to the practical, mundane activities of life are some of the areas to be considered. "Health is not simply the absence of disease, but physical, mental, social and spiritual well-being."[42] Our educators speak about the training of the head, the heart and the hand. Yes, balance and moderation is a valuable concept in psychological health, it is also a crucial concept in Christian living.

Sense of Purpose -- Love of Life, Love of Others

Kinnier says, 'psychologically healthy people believe in something greater than themselves and that they honestly seek and find at least some meaning or purpose in their existence that extends beyond self-preservation and self-gratification.' Christianity above any other philosophy I know gives the individual a purpose for living, a purpose bigger than self. It answers the questions as to who we are, why we are here and where we are heading. It gives satisfying, encouraging answers to these questions. It teaches us to value life, and live it to the fullest. 'I have come,' says Christ, 'that they may have life, and that they may have it to the full.' John 10:10 NIV. Jesus also teaches us not only how to receive and accept his forgiveness, but how to forgive others. The load of hate and the spirit of revenge weigh down many that seek our help. Hate is a heavy psychological load to carry. It saps the energy for living.

When Jesus said that we should love our enemies, he was not only giving sound spiritual advice, he was also sharing a valuable psychological principle that would relieve the suffering of many. When as Christians we share these great themes with troubled people, we are giving not only spiritual help but valuable psychological assistance as well.

Continually Growing or Moving Toward Self- Actualisation

To the Christian, self-actualisation is to be like Jesus Christ. This we know is the work of a lifetime. Theologians refer to it as the process of sanctification. It's continual growth. There is no true self-actualisation apart from Christ. Everything else is inadequate, unsatisfying, dead-end. Augustine was spot-on when he said that we were made with a God-shaped vacuum. Through Christ our self-actualisation goes into eternity. A personal relationship with this person called The Christ opens up dimensions not even dreamt about before knowing him. Paul succinctly puts forward what he understood as the epitome of self-actualisation. He said, "I count not myself to have apprehended: But this one thing I do, forgetting those things which are before, I press toward the mark for the prize of the high calling of God in Christ Jesus." Philippians 3:13,14 KJV.

References:

[1]Nightingale,Earl (1993) **The Essence of Success** p.444 Nightingale-Conant Corporation Illinois

[2]Hart, Dr. Archibald D. (1996) **Habits of the Mind** p. 5 Word Publishing USA

[3]Ibid. p. 185

[4]Hart, Dr. Archibald D. (1996) **Habits of theMind** p.4

[5]Ibid. p.1

[6]Nixon, Richard (1973) **The Lazy Man's Way To Riches** p.161 F.P. Publishing Co. Inc. Carson City, Nevada, USA

[7]Hart, Dr. Archibald D. (1996) **Habits of the Mind** p.161

[8]Nixon, Richard (1973) **The Lazy Man's Way To Riches** p.7

[9]Nightingale, Earl (1993) **The Essence of Success** p. 282

[10]Ibid.

[11]Nigntingale, Earl p. 281

[12]Hart, Dr. Archibald D. (1996) **Habits of the Mind** p.185

[13]Barna, George (1997) **Leaders on Leadership** p.40 Regal Books, Ventura CA USA

[14]Ringer, Robert (1990) **The 10 Habits of Highly Successful People** p.54

[15]Ibid. p.13

[16]Ibid.

[17]Nixon, Richard (1973) **The Lazy Man's Way To Riches** p.16

[18]Ibid. p.141

[19]Ibid. p.163

[20]Nixon,Richard **The Lazy Man's Way To Riches** p.112

[21]Ibid. p.118

[22]Ibid. p.64

[23]Nixon, Richard **The Lazy Man's Way To Riches** p.168

[24]Hart, Dr. Archibald D. **Habits of the Mind** p.176

[25]Ibid. p.170

[26]Nixon, Richard **The Lazy Man's Way To Riches** p.168

[27]Hart, Dr. Archibald D. **Habits of the Mind** p.165

[28]Ibid. p.179

[29]Nixon, Richard **The Lazy Man's Way To Riches** p.123

[30]Ibid. p.129

[31]Ibid. p.131

[32]Maxwell, John C. (1998) **The 21 Irrefutable LAWS OF LEADERSHIP** p.83 Thomas Nelson, Inc. Nashville, Tennessee

[33]

[34]Nixon, Richard **The Lazy Man's Way To Riches** p.183

[35]Maxwell, John C. (1998) **The 21 Irrefutable LAWS OF LEADERSHIP** P.39

[36]McNally, David (1990) **Even Eagles Need a Push** p.121 Dell Publishing New York

[37]Ringer, Robert (1990) **The 10 Habits of Highly Successful People** p.49

[38]Nixon, Richard **The Lazy Man's Way To Riches** p.97

[39]Nightingale, Earl (1993) **The Essence of Success** p.268

[40]Ibid. p.44

[41]Hart, Dr. Archibald D. **Habits of the Mind** p.23

[42]Williams, Hamilton J. (2001) **Take Charge of Your Health** p.15 Total Health Seminars, London

Section Three

SUCCESS WITHIN YOUR GRASP

SUCCESS WITHIN YOUR GRASP

"As-if principle: If you want a quality, act as if you already had it." William James

"It may be all right to be content with what you have; never with what you are." B.C. Forbes

"Knowledge of what is possible is the beginning of happiness." George Santayana

"The future belongs to those who believe in the beauty of their dreams."
Eleanor Roosevelt

Success is No Chance

"Success is not mystery, but simply the result of consistently applying some basic principles. Failure is simply the result of making a few mistakes repeatedly."[1]

"Any human being on earth can be successful if he will decide, once and for all, what it is he wants to accomplish - and really define it, write it out right down to the last comma and period - and then go after it, relentlessly, day after day, week after week, month after month, year after year until it is accomplished."[2]

It was during the days when Kriss Akabusi was at his prime. The time? August 6, 1992. The place? Barcelona. The occasion? The 1992 Olympics. The event? The 400 metres hurdles finals. Kriss Akabusi in his own words said, "I exploded off the blocks... I had barely stepped off the third hurdle and this flash came zooming past me. I thought to myself, my word, you've got to keep your head together, you're obviously having a nightmare." Of course he thought his eyes were playing tricks on him because no one had gone pass him like that in nearly fifteen years. He said however, "all the other runners had the same nightmare," for at the end of the race when they looked up at the screen, a young runner by the name of Kevin Young had blown their socks off by becoming the fastest 400 metres hurdler in history. Akabusi got bronze.

What does all this have to do with the big principle to "write it down?" Well you see when Kevin Young had arrived in his room at the athletes' village at the Olympics he had taped a sheet of paper to the wall on which he had written 46.89 seconds, the time he believed he was capable of running in an Olympic final. It was a time that would have broken a world record established by Ed Moses nine years earlier, and earned him a place in history as the first man to break the 47-second mark in the event.

As it was, the time pinned on the wall was an underestimation. His finishing time was 46.78 seconds. He excelled himself and his expectations. What was a vital part of his success? He had written the time in which he wanted to complete the race on a piece of paper and pinned in on the wall in his room. Everytime he turned in that room, looking back at him was - 46.89 seconds - 46.89 seconds - 46.89 seconds. He got up in the night to go to the bathroom and there it was - 46.89 seconds. He saw it so much that his subconscious mind accepted it as fact and set about to accomplish it. His mind did its work so diligently that he did even better that he thought he would.

"Success is not an accident. It is the result of our attitude and our attitude is a choice. Hence success is a matter of choice not chance."[3]

"Success in life is a matter not so much of talent or opportunity as of concentration and perseverance." C.W. Wendte

What is Success?

"Success is best defined by one's own achievements which may include excellent mental health, physical health, loving relationships - spiritual fulfilment, self-actualisation, material wealth and a rarely achieved peace of mind."[4]

Success is more than earning big money or wielding a lot of power. If you don't believe me take in the end result of the following men.

In 1923, eight of the wealthiest people in the world met. Their combined wealth, it is estimated, exceeded the wealth of the government of the United States at that time. No one in their right mind would have questioned as to whether these were successful men. And yet see what happened to them 25 years later.

1. President of the largest steel company, Charles Schwab, lived on borrowed capital for five years before he died bankrupt.

2. President of the largest gas company, Howard Hubson, went insane.

3. One of the greatest commodity traders, Arthur Cutton, died insolvent.

4. President of the New York Stock Exchange, Richard Whitney, was sent to jail.

5. A member of the President's Cabinet, Albert Fall, was pardoned from jail to go home and die in peace.

6. The greatest "bear" on Wall Street, Jessie Livermore, committed suicide.

7. President of the world's greatest monopoly, Ivar Krueger, committed suicide.

8. President of the Bank of International Settlement, Leon Fraser, committed suicide.

Shiv Khera

"We need two kinds of education. One that teaches us how to make a living and one that teaches us how to live."[5]

"Most people are too busy earning a living to make any money. It is creativity, not hard work, that is at the heart of success in any field of endeavour."[6]

Dreams and Visions

"Where there is no vision, the people perish..." Proverbs 29:18 KJV.

"Successful people are dreamers who have found a dream too exciting, too important, to remain in the realm of fantasy. Day by day, hour by hour, they toil in the service of their dream until they can see it with their eyes and touch it with their hands."[7]

"We grow by dreams. All big men are dreamers, some of us allow our dreams to die, but others nourish and protect them, nurse them through bad days... to sunshine and light which always come. Woodrow Wilson 28th President of the U.S.

Please note this thing about dreams. This is not talking about living in a dream world.
"Dreams are important. However you should not allow your dreams or desires to override reality. In other words your love of truth must be greater than your desire to make your dreams come true."[8]

"Sometimes it's difficult balancing optimism and realism, intuition and planning, faith and fact. But that's what it takes to be effective as a navigating leader."[9] In fact that's what it takes to be successful in life. Successful people are balanced people. Some folk dream too much and end up living in a dream world or reach the place where they substitute the dreams for real accomplishment. Other folk dream too little and as a result live in a harsh world of realism. They pride themselves in being realists. What they really mean is that they are afraid to shoot for the stars because they know before they start that they will never hit a star. Life to such people has very little change; no mystery; no miracle.

"Vision entails change… it's never about maintaining the status quo. Vision is about stretching reality to extend beyond the existing state."[10]

A lofty vision stated clearly contains the power to move mountains!

There Can Be No Success without Clear Goals

The establishment of a goal is the key to successful living. The first step is to define one's objective. Think about this objective every day. Create concrete mental images of the goal, as if you've already accomplished it.[11]

What is important according to scientific evaluation and research, is for you to know what you really want out of life and secondly the ability to use effectively whatever asset you have.

Without clear, well-defined goals, success is impossible.
"Until you write down your dream it is just a dream. Writing it makes it a goal." John Goddard

For years I knew this but I thought if I have my goals well defined in my head then I do not need to write them out. I would go to all kinds of workshops and never pay attention to the writing bits. The important thing, I said to myself, is to understand the concept; to remember the concept. If I can do those two things I do not need to complete the work book assignments. How wrong I was. We cannot fully explain it. But things change when you write. WRITE out your goals. Don't just have it in your head. WRITE IT DOWN. Things were different. Things started changing when I wrote out my goals. Not just goals for one area of your life, but every goal you have for every area of your life.

It is also an important concept to write your goal not just as something you hope to accomplish but as a declaration. For example, let's say your goal is to become financially independent. Don't just state that as a wish, a dream or something you hope to accomplish. Make a declaration. Secondly to say you want to be financially independent is too vague, your mind can hardly work on a goal that vague. Make a very clear declaration and read it every day of your life - morning and evening. So it may look something like this:

I am financially independent. My annual income is £40,200 (£3,350 per month). Now you're on your way to succeeding with that goal. Remember the principle? **"Therefore I tell you, whatever you ask for in prayer, believe that you have received it, and it will be yours."** Mark 11:24 NIV. Of course there is another important principle to note as far as your goals are concerned. Why do you want what you want? What are your motives? The above bible passage should be coupled with another which says **"When you ask, you do not receive, because you ask with wrong motives, that you may spend what you get on your pleasures.** James 4:3 NIV. The King James version uses the word lusts in place of pleasures. In other words the motive is wrong when we want money to spend selfishly on things that will not even benefit us. No person is an Island

"Our success in almost any type of activity will always be in exact ratio to our ability to influence people."[12]
"Our rewards in life will always be in direct proportion to our contribution."[13]

Always give more than you expect to get in return. The person who does more than he/she is paid to do is sooner or later paid willingly far more than he does.

"Your rewards will be determined by the way you do your job, multiplied by the number of people you serve."[14]

"No man can become rich without himself enriching others." Andrew Carnegie

"It's amazing how much can be accomplished if no one cares who gets the credit."[15]

"Force is all-conquering, but its victories are short-lived." Abraham Lincoln.
Examples of this: Adolph Hitler, Idi Amin, Ferdinand Marcos.

"Winners surround themselves with other winners. A winner knows he's a winner. He doesn't need second-raters and yes-men around to feed his ego. He knows he'll win more, and go farther, with associates who not only can keep up with him but who also are capable of teaching him something."[16]

"When you study the lives of successful people, you rarely find a loner -- someone who did it all on his or her own... Success is a co-operative effort... To turn your ideas into reality gain the enthusiastic co-operation of others."[17] Even Jesus Christ surrounded himself with those who would assist Him in accomplishing His mission.

"Help people get what they want and they will help you get what you want. Help enough other people to get what they want out of life and your success is guaranteed."[18]

Let us endeavour so to live that when we come to die even the undertaker will be sorry. Mark Twain

"Loyalty to those with whom we live and work is a prerequisite to top performance.[19]

Integrity

"Integrity in business is the surest way on earth to succeed. Sometimes it might seem that what you're doing is going to cut into profits, but it inevitably ends by increasing profits."[20] **"Let us walk honestly, as in the day..."** Romans 13:13 KJV Transparent goodness is what is being advocated here. If we are people of integrity we will have nothing to hide.

"Be more concerned with your character than with your reputation, because your character is what you really are while your reputation is merely what others think you are."[21] **"A good name is more desirable than great riches..."** (Proverbs 22:1 NIV) This is true but a good character is even better.

"Ability may get you to the top, but it takes character to keep you there."[22]
There are countless people with great ability who continue to flounder around in life. They seem to make it and then crash. They climb again and then crash again. Some are never able to get off the ground. They have the ability but they are missing a crucial ingredient - integrity. I don't need to call any names for you. You doubtlessly know of people of great ability who made

it in society, made it to the top, but could not last up there. Why? They lacked integrity. No matter what your ability, you need character to maintain success. And remember character is not what people think of you - that's your reputation- character is what you are deep down inside. Character is what you are when no one is looking. Or at least when you think no one is looking. You might as well work on your character because someone is always looking. **"The eyes of the Lord are everywhere, keeping watch on the wicked and the good."** Proverbs 15:3 NIV.

And in case like many others you have been trying without success to weed out the negative bits from your character take heart from the wisdom book. **"Can the Ethiopian change his skin or the leopard its spots? Neither can you do good who are accustomed to doing evil."** Jeremiah 13:23 NIV.
"I can do all things through Christ who strengthens me." Philippians 4:13 KJV.
Being a person of integrity is not about pulling one's self up by one's bootstraps but linking our determination to be clean to a source of power that is not only inexhaustible but available.

"The only thing that walks back from the tomb with the mourners and refuses to be buried is the character of the man. What a man is survives him." J.R. Miller

"People will forgive occasional mistakes based on ability, especially if they can see that you're still growing as a leader. But they won't trust someone who has slips in character."[23]

"When we put the well-being of people in first place, we'll never make a mistake." People first, profit last. And the more you do it, the bigger and better your profits become."[24]

Capacity for Hard Work

"Go to the ant thou sluggard; consider her ways, and be wise." Proverbs 6:6 KJV.

"A little sleep, a little slumber, a little folding of the hands to rest - and poverty will come on you like a bandit and scarcity like an armed man. Proverbs 6: 10,11 NIV.

"I'm a great believer in luck, and the harder I work the luckier I get." Stephen Leacock -humorist.

Kemmons Wilson, the founder of Holiday Inns, invited back to give the commencement address to a graduating class at the school he attended said, "I really don't know why I'm here. I never got a degree, and I've only worked half days my entire life. I guess my advice to you is to do the same. Work half days every day. And it doesn't matter which half... the first twelve hours or the second twelve hours."[25]

"Work isn't work if you like it, but a lot of people seem to think that in order to make a living at something, you shouldn't really enjoy doing it... or why would anyone pay you to do it? Not so. Do something you like."[26]

"...you have to be able to work very, very hard, but no, you don't have to approach every assignment in typical 'Type A' full-speed-ahead fashion. Knowing when to throttle down can contribute as much to your performance and your life-span, as knowing when to throttle up."[27]

"Successful people are people who do the things that unsuccessful people refuse to do. They understand that every task they handle is a self-portrait of the person who performed it, and they have committed themselves to autograph every job with excellence."[28]

"It's easy to succeed today. We have no competition. If you want to get ahead in life, go the extra mile. There is no competition on the extra mile. Are you willing to do a little more than you get paid for?[29] **"If someone forces you to go one mile, go with him two miles."** Matthew 5:41 NIV

Remember every time you go the extra mile you place someone under obligation to you.

Between 90-99% of what we do every day is habitual in behaviour. The difference between being successful and not being successful really depends on those habits. We have to change our failure habits into success habits and that takes time and constant reinforcement. Psychiatrists tell us it takes the average person about 30 repetitions of an activity to turn it into a habit... and the more of you that is involved, the quicker you will develop the new habit."[30]

Some Negative Mindsets to Avoid

" If you keep too busy learning the tricks of the trade, you may never learn the trade."[31] So many people today hold on to the mistaken belief that one has to know some tricks in order to succeed in life. And so instead of using their brainpower to provide a real benefit or supply a real need, they are constantly seeking to discover ways of cutting corners or conning people. The question is how many opportunities would you get to con the same person? Only one. Unless the person is a real dunce. And then a person who has been 'taken for a ride' doesn't keep it to himself. It therefore becomes self-defeating to whatever business you're in to be less than honest with your customers.

"If you keep on saying things are going to be bad, you have a good chance of being a prophet." Isaac Bashevis Singer This is because every cell in your body is listening to everything you say. You say it often enough and the body prepares itself to carry out what it interprets as your wishes.

"The something-for-nothing urge is part of the human psyche and is based on sheer self-delusion."[32] Where in nature or in society do you see that law being played out? You won't find it. And yet so many believe it and spend their entire lives hoping to strike it rich by putting that make-belief law into operation.

"Some people stop working as soon as they find a job."[33] They do just barely enough so as not to get fired. And they think that they're saving themselves and nobody is noticing. Everybody including the boss knows the clock-watcher, the one who will do absolutely nothing if he can get away with it. And you will be rewarded accordingly.

People today who complain about a lack of opportunity are generally the kind of people who have the mistaken idea that the world owes them a living. They're generally the people who sit around waiting for something wonderful to happen to them, with no particular effort on their part. In fact, many people still hold the mistaken idea that it's not what you know but who you know. They couldn't be more wrong, and as long as they cling to this worn-out, old alibi, they're their own worst enemy."[34]

"Losers want security, winners seek opportunity. Losers are more afraid of life than death."[35] Neither a dog nor a mule have any respect for the person who fears it.

Misfortune seldom tangles with the person whose constant bodyguards are hope and faith. "...putting on the breastplate of **faith** ..., and for a helmet, the **hope** of salvation. 1 Thessalonians 5:8 KJV. "Which **hope** we have as an anchor of the soul..." Hebrews 6:19 KJV.

Perspective

"Every successful person keeps his problems in proper perspective and makes it a habit to search immediately for the offsetting positives in every negative situation."[36]
It's different with losers. To the loser every difficulty is a crisis; every molehill is a mountain; every challenge a disaster. If you have developed the bad habit of this approach to life, it is just that, a bad habit. Get a hold of yourself. The next time life throws up one of its challenges some people call problems remind yourself - this too shall pass. I will survive this. Life will continue after this.

St. Paul grasped the success principle when he exposed his attitude on challenges by saying: **"We are hard-pressed on every side, but not crushed; perplexed, but not in despair; persecuted but not abandoned; struck down, but not destroyed."** 2 Corinthians 4:8,9 NIV. No wonder no one could stop him. No wonder when wicked men stoned him and then took him and threw him outside the city thinking he was dead, after a while Paul got up and walked back into the city. Acts 14:19,20

Accept the fact that every living being has what most people refer to as problems. To pursue a problem-free life is to run after an elusive fantasy, a mirage in the desert.

You will notice if you take time to observe that every difficulty has a limited life span. Your storm too will pass. Your problem will be resolved.

Every problem holds positive possibilities and will change you. It's up to you to turn your pain into profanity or poetry.

When you can't solve a problem- manage it. Some of you may be saying that some problems go on and on - the damage is permanent. That's true. You can still get the upper hand if you manage such a situation. If your leg is amputated, you can't grow it back - but you can manage it by determining to walk better, more smoothly, more quickly than anybody else could imagine.

"Man is the only "animal" who can laugh at himself. He can choose not to see every problem, every unfair act, and every negative situation as monumental in importance."[37]

You've got to train yourself to see more than others see, to see further than others see and see before others do. This constitutes greatness.

Internal Motivation

"I couldn't wait for success - so I went ahead without it." Jonathan Winters

So many people know what they need to do; they know that action is needed today but they sit around waiting they say for the right circumstances, waiting for their luck to change. But high achievers just get on with it and do what needs to be done. As a result success catches up with them.

Successful people compete against themselves. They better their own record and keep improving constantly. Losers keep competing against the neighbours, friends, enemies, sometimes against people in their own household.

Low achievers must have motivation from outside of themselves. Something or someone has to push them, prod them, plead with them, pamper them. Or they attempt to motivate themselves by competing against others. This kind of motivation leads some folk to accomplish quite a lot but it has within it the seeds of its own destruction. It is not wholesome motivation and it does not last.

Internal motivation is lasting, because it comes from within and translates into self-motivation. Motivation needs to be identified and constantly strengthened to succeed. Keep your goals in front of you and read them morning and evening.[38]

"All great leaders and teachers throughout history have concluded that one must be internally driven in order to be a success."[39]

"Destiny is not a matter of chance; it is a matter of choice. It is not a thing to be waited for; it is a thing to be achieved." William Jennings Bryan
"There is nothing capricious in nature. Nature will not plant a burning desire in your mind if you do not have the innate capability to achieve that desire." Ralph Waldo Emerson

"Just a small fire cannot give much heat, a weak desire cannot produce great results"[40]

What and how much you accomplish in life may be directly

related to the strength of your desire. If it's something important to you, I mean really important, then stay with it, build the fire, see it in your imagination, feel it, smell it, touch it, taste it - this is the only way to achieve great results. That weak, anaemic wanting to or wishing to will accomplish absolutely nothing. Engage your emotions! Generate some living colour into your life and stop forever living in greys and browns. Some of you may have to practice again how to get excited about life.

"Nothing can withstand the power of the human will if it is willing to stake its very existence to the extent of its purpose." Benjamin Disraeli

"Everything can and will be changed, improved. The only thing you can count on for certain is change. Don't wait for it - be in the forefront - help to bring it about." [41]

The average person puts only 25% of his energy and ability into his work. The world takes off its hat to those who put in more than 50% of their capability, and stands on its head for those few and far between souls who devote 100%. Andrew Carnegie

"Make no little plans; they have no magic to stir men's blood… make big plans, aim high in hope and work." Daniel H. Burnham

Many people are suffering from the poverty of expectation. Your life will come pretty close to matching your expectations.

Self-esteem is how we feel about ourselves. Self-esteem is a major component in determining success or failure. Unless you perceive yourself as worthwhile, you cannot have high self-esteem. High self-esteem leads to a happy, gratifying and purposeful life. People with high self-esteem grow in conviction, competence and willingness to accept responsibility. They face life with optimism, have better relationships and fulfilling lives. They are motivated and ambitious. They are more sensitive.

One great booster of self-esteem is the fact that Jesus Christ died for us. One inspired author says if you were the only person on earth Jesus Christ, the Son of God would still have left the glories of heaven and suffered and died for you, just for you. Now that's awesome to contemplate! It therefore doesn't matter who you are, what you have done or how little you think of yourself the whole point of Jesus' mission was to give you back your self worth. You're valuable in his sight. You're somebody. You've got royal blood in your veins. You're a child of God. Terrible things may have been done to you in your childhood. You may have been made to feel like utter garbage, but Jesus Christ came to give you back your self-respect. Don't go through the rest of your life rubbishing what He has done for you and holding on to your damaged self-esteem as if it's precious. Let it go and hold on to the thought that you're precious in the eyes of God. And that's worth more than what a million other people can say to you or about you.

We transfer our unconscious self-appraisal to others and they respond to us accordingly. Human beings cannot perform beyond the boundaries of their self-concept, whatever it may be.[42]

Growth

"It's what you learn after you know it all that counts."[43]

"Happy, successful people don't go through life, they grow through life."[44]

Learn to do something better than anyone else can do it and you can forget your financial problems.

The person who learns while he earns is being paid to go to school.

There can be no success without growth and growth happens in one of three ways:
By starting something new: Make a list of the things you need to start doing.
By stopping something you are presently doing: Make a list of the things you need to stop doing.
By learning from the mistakes we make: List three mistakes you have made recently and then suggest the three most important lessons you can learn from those mistakes.[45]

"That which you can confront you can control; that which you cannot confront will control you."[46]
It's amazing how ingenious human beings can become in finding ways to avoid facing up to certain realities and truths. If you continue to do that you will remain a little mental and spiritual dwarf for the rest of your life. No growth can take place if you refuse to face up to issues in your life. Putting it off to some later date won't make it easier either. In fact it often becomes more complicated and deep-rooted. The sooner you face up to those issues that are causing havoc in your life the sooner you can move on and grow and glow.

"Learn as if you were to live forever; Live as if you were to die tomorrow."[47]

Learn as if you were to live forever: Never stop reading and seeking to know, to expand your horizon. Remember you're never too old to feel a little younger. Many people allow themselves to deteriorate mentally because they feel they're too old to be learning new things. I met a man in his sixties and was sharing with him some health principles that would assist him in accessing a higher quality of life. "Oh, I'm too old for that" he said, " I'm just waiting for them to put me in me box." How sad I thought. Here was a "dead" man walking about. He was not suffering from any debilitating disease. He was up and about and still fairly alert, but all his life consisted of was waiting to be placed in a box.

Live as if you were to die tomorrow: This simply means use time wisely. Don't keep putting off for tomorrow those things that you know need to be done today. So many regrets I have heard along the lines: "Oh if only I could get just one more opportunity to let her know how much I loved her." But alas it was too late. Work from a written list of priorities and do what is important to be done today.

"Striving for perfection is neurotic; striving for excellence is progress, because there is nothing that can't be done better or improved."[48]

Using your Time For Success

"Most people spend more time planning a party or vacation than planning their lives."[49]

"The more a person is frustrated and failing, the more willing, even anxious, he is to waste time on petty matters."[50]

Most people are caught up in the thick of thin things. Most of us are drowning in a sea of unimportant to marginally important papers. A little discipline like allowing yourself to handle a piece of paper only once can have a major impact on the quality of your results.

"Procrastination is the greatest destroyer of success that I know."[51]
Text --- a little bit of … and poverty sneaks up.

If it's worth doing, it's worth doing NOW, unless that in which you are involved right now has a definite higher priority. Don't argue with yourself, don't make excuses, don’t accept the reasoning that you would do it later. Do it now. You won't believe how much you will get done and how much more successful your life would be if you follow this simple rule.

"We work hardest and most efficiently when we know there's a definite time element involved."[52] Set time limits for the simplest of jobs and be sure to set time limits for the important things you need to do.

Remember that work expands to fill the time available for its completion. Set a deadline or you will be working forever on a single project.

"Taking no action is the greatest danger of all."[53]

Developing the discipline of using time wisely is one of the single greatest principles that will change your life and put you on the road of success. The average person has no concept of how much time he flitters away on absolute time wasters and marginally important matters. Many will be shocked to discover how many hours they spend watching television and most of that not even programmes that they have made any decision to watch. People generally do not understand the tremendous difference two hours of concentrated effort a day in a particular area can make to their lives. They honestly feel they don't have time and yet allow hours to slip away unnoticed by the minutes.

Some Other Principles to Note

It is well established that the largest and most powerful locomotive in the world can be held in place by a one-inch block of wood. Placed in front of the eight drive wheels of the locomotive, the block will hold it completely motionless. Yet that same locomotive, with a full head of steam, can crash through a steel-reinforced concrete wall that is five feet thick. That is what getting the action habit can do for us!"[54] However small the action, don't wait any longer, get moving on that project, get moving on that new habit you want to develop, get moving on that attitude. Do something right now that will send a signal to your subconscious that you mean business.

"It's a lack of discretion to announce your plans to the world. There are too many envious and malevolent people out there that just love to see you trip. Avoid revealing the heart of your enterprise to more people than are absolutely necessary to bring about its success."[55] A dream is especially vulnerable and fragile in its early stages. If you expose that dream to the wrong people they will kill it before it has time to even develop some immunity to all the dream-killing viruses around.

"You have not only the right, but also the personal responsibility to think in a cool and calm way about any major investment you are asked to make. Never make a significant deal that is proposed to you, a deal that is going to involve your commitment to spend your own money, on the spur of the moment. There is no more certain recipe for disaster than a decision based on emotion."[56]

"Successful people have to continue to develop a sense of humour. They seldom take themselves seriously, but they take their work seriously. They tend to be easy going, easy to talk to, comfortable people who believe that ostentation and putting on airs are signs of mental immaturity."[57]

"Maturity starts when you accept that there is no one out there to rescue you, so you plan to rescue yourself."[58]

"Touch a thistle timidly, and it pricks you; grasp it boldly, and its spines crumble. All problems become smaller if you don't dodge them but confront them." William

"Winning is an event. Being a winner is a spirit."[59]

You've got to give up to go up

"Many people today want to climb up the corporate ladder because they believe that freedom and power are the prizes waiting at the top. They don't realise that the true nature of leadership is really sacrifice and sacrifice is an ongoing process, not a one-time payment."[60]

"Anytime you know that the step is right, don't hesitate to make a sacrifice"[61] If you put your foot to the plow and turn back you're not fit for the kingdom. Luke 9:62 The kingdom referred to here is the kingdom of God, but it holds true for the kingdom of success here and now, the kingdom of taking charge of your life and making a worthwhile contribution.

Usually the higher the person has climbed, the greater the sacrifices he has made. If you're not willing to make sacrifices then forget about success and continue living your boring, colourless, scraping-through life.

"For everything you have missed, you have gained something else; and for everything you gain, you lose something." Ralph Waldo Emerson

References -

[1]Khera, Shiv (1998) **You Can Win** p.34 Simon & Schuster Pte Ltd. Singapore

[2]Nightingale, Earl (1993) **The Essence of Success** p.385 Nigntingale-Conant Corporation, Illinois

[3]Khera, Shiv (1998) **You Can Win** p.33

[4]Nixon, Richard G. (1973) **The Lazy Man's Way To Riches** p.4 F.P. Publishing Co. Inc. Carson City, Nevada, USA

[5]Khera, Shiv (1998) **You Can Win** p.190

[6]Ringer, Robert (1990) **The 10 Habits of Highly Successful People** p.147 Advantage Quest Publications, Malaysia

[7]Nightingale, Earl (1993) **The Essence of Success** p.401

[8]Ringer, Robert (1990) **The 10 Habits of Highly Successful People** p.34

[9]Maxwell, John C. (1998) **The 21 Irrefutable LAWS OF LEADERSHIP** p.39 Thomas Nelson, Inc, Nashville, Tennessee

[10]Barna, George (1992) **The Power of Vision** p.29 Regal Books Ventura, CA 93006

[11]Kiev, Ari (1997) **Strategy for Daily Living**

[12]Nightingale, Earl (1993) **The Essence of Success** p.225

[13]Ibid. p233

[14]Nightingale, Earl (1993) **The Essence of Success** p.234

[15]Wooden, John (1988) **They Call Me Coach** p.104 Contemporary Publishing Co. Chicago, Illinois

[16]Mackay, Harvey (1989) **Swim With the Sharks** p.121 Sphere Books Ltd. Shoe Lane, London

[17]Nixon, Richard G. (1973) **The Lazy Man's Way To Riches** p.191

[18]Ibid.

[19]Ziglar, Zig (1986) **Top Performance** p.103 The Berkley Publishing Group New York

[20]Nightingale,Earl (1993) **The Essence of Success** p.52

[21]Wooden, John (1988) **They Call Me Coach** p.68

[22]Ibid. p.152

[23]Maxwell, John C. (1998) **The 21 Irrefutable LAWS OF LEADERSHIP** p.58

[24]Nightingale, Earl (1993) **The Essence of Success** p.52

[25]Mackay, Harvey (1998) **Swim With the Sharks** p.145

[26]Ibid. p.199
[27]Ibid.p.146 p.247
[28]Ziglar,Zig (1986) **Top Performance**
[29]Khera, Shiv (1998) **You Can Win** p.54
[30]Nixon, Richard G. (1993) **The Lazy Man's Way To Riches** p.21
[31]Wooden, John (1988) **They Call Me Coach** p.109
[32]Ringer, Robert (1990) **The 10 Habits of Highly Successful People** p.19
[33]Khera, Shiv (1998) **You Can Win** p.49
[34]Nightingale, Earl (1993) **The Essence of Success** p.404
[35]Khera, Shiv (1998) **You Can Win** p.46
[36]Ringer, Robert (1990) **The 10 Habits of Highly Successful People** p.70
[37]Ibid. p.72
[38]Khera, Shiv (1998) **You Can Win** p.87
[39]Ibid. p.94
[40]Ibid. p.44
[41]Nightingale, Earl (1993) **The Essence of Success** p.130
[42]Khera, Shiv (1998) **You Can Win** p.94
[43]Wooden, John (1988) **They Call Me Coach** p.125
[44]Ziglar, Zig (1986) **Top Performance** p.97
[45]Nixon, Richard G. (1993) **The Lazy Man's Way To Riches** p.12
[46]Ringer, Robert (1990) **The 10 Habits of Highly Successful People** p.215
[47]Wooden, John (1988) **They Call Me Coach** p.43
[48]Khera, Shiv (1998) **You Can Win** p.36
[49]Ibid. p.69
[50]Ringer, Robert (1990) **The 10 Habits of Highly Successful People** p.125
[51]Nixon, Richard G. (1993) **The Lazy Man's Way To Riches** p.121
[52]Nightingale, Earl (1993) **The Essence of Success** p.140
[53]Ringer, Robert (1990) **The 10 Habits of Highly Successful People** p.230
[54]Ziglar, Zig (1986) **Top Performance** p.249
[55]Ringer, Robert (1990) **The 10 Habits of Highly Successful People** p.118
[56]Mackay, Harvey (1989) **Swim With the Sharks** p.91
[57]Nightingale, Earl (1993) **The Essence of Success** p.378
[58]Nixon, Richard G. (1993) **The Lazy Man's Way To Riches** p.101
[59]Khera, Shiv (1998) **You Can Win** p.214
[60]Maxwell, John C. (1998) **The 21 Irrefutable LAWS OF LEADERSHIP** P.188
[61]Ibid. p.189

Section Four

HAPPINESS WITHIN YOUR GRASP

HAPPINESS WITHIN YOUR GRASP!

Happiness is the inner music of the soul.

He is happy who finds something he loves doing most that allows him to forget himself.

"Success and happiness go hand in hand. Success is getting what you want and happiness is wanting what you get."[1]

"Happy is he whose help is the God of Jacob, whose hope is in the Lord his God, the maker of heaven and earth..."
Psalm 146:5,6 NIV.

Happiness - A By-product

"Those only are happy who have their minds fixed on some object other than their own happiness: on happiness of others, on the improvement of mankind, even on some art or pursuit, followed not as a means, but as itself an ideal end. Aiming thus at something else, they find happiness by the way." John Stuart Mill

"Happiness is a by-product of a meaningful life."[2] "Money must be a side effect of a higher purpose."[3]

"The happiest people are usually the busiest people, and almost always those whose business consists of serving others in some way. By losing themselves in what they're doing and where they're going, happiness quietly joins them and becomes part of them."[4]

The healthy person finds happiness in helping others. He is selfish in a healthy way, a way that is beneficial to him and to society too becausc he gets his pleasure from the pleasure of other people.

Yet it calls for sensible balance --"don't be so much to everyone else that you become nothing to yourself."[5]

Happiness is something that must be learned and practised if we're to become skilled at it.

Happiness is a condition rather than a destination. It cannot be pursued.

Again and again, no matter where we turn we come back to this biblical principle of life -- to find life which incorporates lasting happiness you must first learn how to lose it in service it to others or in a cause that will benefit people. The happiest people I know are those who spend themselves making others happy. And the most miserable people I know are those who shut themselves away behind high physical and psychological fences. In an effort to shut out others they shut out happiness also.

It's Not Out There!

Changing your external circumstances will not necessarily bring happiness and seldom does. Nothing external, in and of itself can bring genuine success and happiness. Changing your circumstances won't change who you are. Only you can do that. Permanent, powerful, lasting change can only come from within.

"Most people are about as happy as they make up their mind to be. Abraham Lincoln - 16th President of the U.S.

"It is not easy to find happiness in ourselves and it is not possible to find it elsewhere. Agnes Repplier

No Happiness without Balance

Happy people live balanced lives. They don't become workaholics, fanatics, crash dieters, food bingers or pleasure addicts. They're active physically, socially, mentally and spiritually.

A happy person has a low degree of self-conflict. He is not at war with himself. His personality is integrated. He therefore does not burn up all his energy fighting battles with himself. He uses that energy for living purposefully. This is why it's absolutely necessary to determine what your values are and then live them. You can't be happy otherwise.

"The mature person strives for strength -- strength of purpose, strength of mind, and strength of character. Only these can give us peace and serenity, joy and accomplishment."[6] You develop strength of purpose, mind and character by discovering who you are, why you are here, where you are going and how to get there. There is no other source I know which answers all those questions satisfactorily than the Bible. But a cursory glance through will only confuse you more. As the Bible itself says you've got to search it as if you're mining for gold and hidden treasure. Only to such a person it yields its awesome treasures.

Perspective

"Higher than the highest human thought can reach is God's ideal for His children." Ellen White

"No plan can humanly be conceived that can outshine the one He has divinely created for you."[7]

People who have found happiness are usually more flexible and spontaneous. They are not rigid in their attitudes and plans. They are able to view life as an adventure.

Happy people have very rich relationships with other people. They're not comparing, competing or criticising. They almost never overreact to negative behaviours, criticism, or human weaknesses. They do not label, stereotype, categorise or prejudge. They're quick to forgive and don't carry grudges. They heed the great wisdom book when it says:
"...Everyone should be quick to listen, slow to speak and slow to become angry." James 1:19 NIV. **"In your anger do not sin. Do not let the sun go down while you are still angry."** Ephesians 4:26 This is revealing. Anger is not an evil emotion. The advice is however, to watch what you do with your anger, therein may lie the evil. Secondly don't allow your anger to seethe, deal with it, resolve it, and do so as far as possible before the day ends.

Have you ever noticed how most people seem to be waiting to be happy in the future? The fact is that most of the ingredients necessary for happiness are present in the lives of most people every day. They are things and conditions for which we need not wait. And most of them are things we're so used to; we take them for granted. They're people with whom we live and work, our children, our hopes; there's the anticipation of the day and what it will bring; the opportunity to work well and honestly so that we can take pride and satisfaction from it and by so doing enjoy our leisure and our rest.

Some people are always planning to be happy in the future. It's like the person who puts the best china and silver and linen away for some future, or very special time, and dies before any of it is ever used. Or it's like the person who puts seat covers in his car and thus, passes on, to the second person to buy it, brand new upholstery that he himself never used or enjoyed.

"And so, millions of people with the miracle of sight never really see the world about them until it's practically too late; millions with the inborn capacity to love, and to know the joy that loving brings, wait too long to express it. They live through the years without really being aware of their days, or the riches that are passing through their hands."[8]

"It is only when life is threatened that a conception of its value begins to dawn on the average person."[9]

The thoughtful person finds happiness in just being alive. He enjoys walking on a sunny day... but he likes walking in the rain, too. He can find happiness from the sound of the surf, or the crackling of a fire.

The person who has an awareness of living finds happiness. "It means being aware that you are alive at this moment, and that the world and people are interesting enough at any time so that we need not waste so precious a thing as time, in boredom."[10]

"If the course to which you're holding is right, everything else you want will come as by-products."[11]

Many people misunderstand this thing called money. Some feel that money will bring them happiness. They're wrong of course. There are others who believe that you can't be rich and happy, it's either one or the other, they're also wrong. "Some of the most miserable people I've known have been millionaires. They were miserable because they thought that money would make them happy. But they weren't miserable because they were rich. If they lost their money, they'd just be poor and miserable."[12]

There are many that mistakenly believe that the Bible says that money is the root of all evil. That's a misquote that is almost universal. What the Bible does say is that "the love of money is a root of all kinds of evil." 1Timothy 6:10 NIV. "The **love** of money." That's quite different, isn't it?

You Won't Find It This Way

The miserable person who turns inward upon himself doesn't have much in the wisdom department, or he'd never do it; and as a result, he doesn't have much to turn inward upon. He finds a kind of vacuum, and he must then invent things. He invents things like "the world is against him" - which is the worst kind of conceit. The world isn't against him- it doesn't even know he exists - and as a result, it ignores him completely.[13]

"Many of our miseries are merely comparative; we are often made unhappy, not by the presence of any real evil, but by the absence of some fictitious good." Samuel Johnson

"Human beings have the strangest and most perverse tendency to take the best parts of life for granted."[14]

Guilt is a great drawback in the search for success. The greatest wisdom book tells us how to get rid of guilt. We will come to this again but at this time immerse yourself in the satisfaction of this: "**You (God) will again have compassion on us, you will tread our sin underfoot and hurl all our iniquities in the depths of the sea.**" Micah 7:19 NIV. Keep in mind that there are parts of the ocean that are seven miles deep. A lot of water is on top of it -- let it go!

"The miserable, unhappy people who cause so much misery and unhappiness in others are the self-centred people... people who worry constantly about what they're getting, rather than what they're giving; and the world is full of them, unfortunately. We see their harried, unhappy, furtive, ferret-like faces everywhere, pushing, their grasping hands extended. They fear life, they fear death. They are the pitiful caricatures of humanity. And they pay a terrible price for their ignorance."[15]

The Happiness Test

On a scale of 1 to 7 indicate how much you agree or disagree with each of the following statements.

1. Strongly disagree
2. Disagree
3. Slightly disagree
4. Neither agree nor disagree
5. Slightly agree
6. Agree
7. Strongly agree

- In most ways my life is close to my ideal.
- The conditions of my life are excellent.
- I am satisfied with my life.
- So far I have the important things I want in life.
- If I could live my life again, I would change almost nothing.

5-9	Extremely dissatisfied with your life.
10-14	Very dissatisfied
15-19	Slightly dissatisfied
20	Neutral
21-25	Somewhat dissatisfied
26-30	Very satisfied
31-35	Extremely satisfied

Most people score in the 21-25 range.

In a Gallop poll of 18 nations, the Icelandic were the world's happiest people. The British ranked sixth. 66% of Britons are satisfied with their personal lives.

Reader'sDigest
December '97

Happiness knows no gender.
Happiness doesn't depend on age.
Wealth does not beget happiness.
A survey by Forbes magazine's list of the 100 wealthiest Americans, found that the privileged are not much happier than average people.
Happiness and marriage go together. Most people are happier attached than unattached. Truly the Creator said: "It is not good that man should be alone." Genesis 2:18 KJV.

David Myers offers these steps:

1. Savour the moment.
2. Take control of your time.
3. Accentuate the positive. It boosts the body's immune system and healing process.
4. Give priority to close relationships. Those who could name five close friends were
   60% more likely to be very happy than people who couldn't name any. (US National Opinion Research Centre). Act happy. People who put on a happy face really do feel better. It seems that facial muscles used to smile trigger happy feelings in the brain.
   "A cheerful heart is good medicine, but a crushed spirit dries up the bones." Proverbs 17:22 NIV.
5. Don't vegetate. Get involved. Don't park in front of the Television.
6. Get moving. Get moderate exercise.
7. Get enough rest.
8. Take care of the soul. People who are actively religious are happier than those who aren't.

(Princeton Religious Research Centre and Gallup)

A story is told of a horse that had shied when he came to a stump on the road. Subsequently, every time the horse came to that same stump, he shied. The farmer dug the stump out, burned it, and levelled the old road. Yet, for 12 years, every time the horse passed the place where the former stump was, he shied. The horse was shying at the memory of a stump.

There is no block to your happiness save in your own thought life and mental imagery.

You Must Find Your Purpose in Order to Be Happy

"What man needs is not a tensionless state, but rather the striving and struggling of some goal worthy of him."

"Many persons have a wrong idea of what constitutes true happiness. It is not attained through self-gratitude but through fidelity to a worthy purpose." Helen Keller

What is my purpose in life? This is Life's most powerful question.

How do you discover your purpose? Start with identifying the things in life that make you experience a deep down feeling of satisfaction, that make you come alive, that make you say "Yes!"

Keep in mind what Victor Frankl said, "we don't invent our mission; we detect it. It's within us waiting to be realised."

"Existence is a strange bargain. Life owes us little; we owe it everything. The only true happiness comes from squandering ourselves for a purpose." William Cowper

Each of us has been uniquely created to be and do certain things -- our purpose. It's a sense of destiny... You'll never be happy or find that inner peace and joy of life, until you find and follow your own powerful purpose."[16]

"Purpose gives meaning, power, focus and direction to your goals and therefore to your life."[17]

"More men fail through lack of purpose than lack of talent." Billy Sunday

"A life isn't significant except for its impact on other lives."
Jackie Robinson

"I believe the purpose of life is to be a growing, contributing involved human being and that life is at its best when you are willingly and happily contributing to other people and society."[18]

Your goals are not your purpose. Your purpose must have a people connection.

"Purpose is where to go and goals are how to get there. A purpose is not a goal. Your purpose can never be reached and then checked off like a goal."[19]

When you don't have a purpose you may experience an empty life without a sense of joy and meaning. The daily objective becomes just a struggle to solve one problem after another to survive. This leads to disease, alcohol and drug abuse, crime, and becoming a burden to family and society.

"The secret of achieving inner peace lies in understanding our inner core values -- those things in our lives that are most important to us -- and then seeing that they are reflected in the daily events of our lives. In other words, doing a better joy of managing our time is meaningless unless we are managing it to accomplish those things that are of greatest importance in our lives."[20]

Actively create that life rather than be created by the circumstances around you. Instead of being manipulated by various life-moulds, manage your own life by making your life happen. It's called living your life on purpose![21]

"Higher than the highest human thought can reach is God's ideal for His children."
Ellen G. White

"No plan can humanly be conceived that can outshine the one He (God) has divinely created for you."[21]

References: -

[1]Khera, Shiv (1998) **You Can Win** p35 Simon & Schuster Pte Ltd Singapore

[2]Ringer, Robert (1990) **The 10 Habits of Highly Successful People** p.87 Advantage Quest Publications, Malaysia

[3]Ibid.

[4]Nightingale, Earl (1993) **The Essence of Success** p.416

[5]Ringer, Robert (1990) **The 10 Habits of Highly Successful People** p.142

[6]Nightingale, Earl (1993) **The Essence of Success** p.44

[7]Barna, George (1992) **The Power of Vision** p.72 Regal Books, Ventura, CA 93006

[8]Nightingale, Earl (1993) **The Essence of Success** p.436

[9]Ibid.

[10]Ibid. p.433

[11]Nightingale, Earl (1993) **The Essence of Success** p.422

[12]Nixon, Richard G. (1973) **The Lazy Man's Way To Riches** p.147 F.P. Publishing Co. Inc. Carson City, Nevada, USA

[13]Nightingale, Earl (1993) **The Essence of Success** p.420

[14]Ibid. p.421

[15]Ibid. p.416

[16]Nixon, Richard G. (1973) **The Lazy Man's Way To Riches** p.10

[17]Ibid. p.19

[18]Ibid. p.90

[19]Nixon, Richard G. (1973) **The Lazy Man's Way To Riches** p. 101

[20]Smith, Hyrum W. (1995) **The 10 Natural Laws of Successful Time & Life Management** p. 3 Nicholas Brealey Publishing, London

[21]Nixon, Richard G. (1973) **The Lazy Man's Way To Riches** p.9

[22]Barna, George (1992) **The Power of Vision** p.72

Section Five

DISCIPLINE - DETERMINATION - PERSEVERANCE

DISCIPLINE - DETERMINATION -PERSEVERANCE

"First say to yourself what you would be; and then do what you have to do." Epictetus

"Give me where to stand and I will move the earth." Archimedes

There are some defeats more triumphant than victories." Michel De Montaigne

"Never a person less free that when he is enslaved by his emotions." Robert Ringer

"...I do not consider myself yet to have taken hold of it. But one thing I do: Forgetting what is behind and straining toward what is ahead, I press on toward the goal to win the prize for which God has called me..." Philippians 3:13,14 NIV.

"Therefore I do not run like a man running aimlessly; I do not fight like a man beating the air. No, I beat my body and make it my slave so that after I have preached to others, I myself will not be disqualified for the prize." 1 Corinthians 9:26,27 NIV.

Nothing is Accomplished Without Discipline

Self-discipline is about acting on your intellectual conclusions and overriding your instinctive desire for instant gratification. A truly self-disciplined person is able to do this even when his emotions are running high."[1]

Self-discipline is a learned art, and to master this art requires two steps:

1. Consistently analyse the probable, long-term consequences of your actions.
2. Be tenacious in acting in accordance with what you have determined to be in your long-term best interests.

"No horse gets anywhere until he is harnessed.
No steam or gas ever drives anything until it is confined.
No Niagara is ever turned into light and power until it is tunnelled.
No life ever grows great until it is focused, dedicated, disciplined."
Harry Emerson Fosdick

"Winning in life comes when we do not succumb to what we want to do, but do what ought to be done. That requires discipline."[2]

"Be first master of yourself, and only then a master of others."
Baltasar Gracian.

Freedom comes from triumphing over your emotions and proving to yourself that you can be master of your destiny."[3]

The experts say that each of us has deep reservoirs of ability which we habitually fail to use simply because we fail to develop ourselves to our true stature.[4]

Only a few exceptional persons make any serious demands of themselves. The rest quit and sit down, gasping at the first sign of fatigue, thus failing to tap into the 'second wind.'

"Evidently, we stockpile reserves of energy we don't ordinarily use. And these reserves will go to work only when we demand enough of ourselves."[5]

I have personally experienced this when I run marathons. I am no top-flight athlete. I consider myself a fitness jogger. Whenever I run the London marathon, after the first two or three miles I feel like I can't even reach mile 5 far more mile 26! But I do not listen to my body. I persist. I make serious demands on my body and then something wonderful happens - my body begins to tap into the 'second wind', my breathing smoothes out, I feel comfortable and I know I can make it. But that's not the end. It happens again after mile 16 and again after mile 22. After that it's not muscle that takes me in. It's my mind. So it is in all areas of life. Learn to make serious demands on your self and you will be surprised at what can be accomplished after the point when you think you've had it.

No Success without Determination

"Don't tell me you 'can't.' What you really mean is you 'won't.'"[6]

"All things are possible until they are proved impossible - and even the impossible may only be so as of now." Pearl S. Buck

"Some men succeed because they are destined to, but most men because they are determined to." Anonymous

"If you don't learn to anticipate and rehearse success, you rob yourself of the energy and determination that you need to be successful."[7]

You've Got to Develop Staying Power

Jesus replied, 'No one who puts his hand to the plow and looks back is fit for service in the kingdom of God.' Luke 9:62 NIV

"Persistence is a decision. It is a commitment to finish what you start."[8]

"That which we persist in doing becomes easier to do. It's not that the nature of the thing has changed, but that our ability to do it has increased." Ralph Waldo Emerson

Be consistently focused. Dabblers are rarely successful. It's when you focus totally, intensely, and consistently on one project - a project that has the potential to yield a worthwhile payoff - that you have the greatest chance for success.[9]

"He knows not his own strength that hath not met adversity." Ben Johnson (1573-1637)

"Life has a way of testing your desires by setting some obstacles in your way. Too many people give up at the first set back."[10]

" Perseverance is probably the most powerful success tool known to man... Perseverance means being able to handle massive rejection, massive disappointment, and massive frustration. It's what makes you persist long after the other guy has given up... Perseverance is a trait so powerful that it can overcome almost any deficiency."[11] Most of the great success stories are not about people who had exceptional ability or talent. What made them astoundingly successful was their ability to keep going, putting one foot in front the other when the average person had given up long ago. It's a different matter if you doubt that what you're doing or where you're going is the right direction. But once you have done your homework and you know that you're headed in the right direction, what are you stopping for? Keep going. That's how people succeed. It is called perseverance.

"What appears to be genius is often nothing more than the art of taking pains." Claude Hopkins

Noah Webster

It took Noah Webster 36 years to compile *Webster's Dictionary*. Today we live in a world of instant gratification. Folk can't stick with something for 36 days far more 36 years.

Have you grown up in a negative and even hostile environment? Have other people told you that you would never amount to anything? Have you felt the odds to succeed in life were against you? You are not alone.
"In terms of what we have available to us to assist us in coping or to do more than cope, someone said:
'To each is given a bag of tools,
A shapeless mass, and a book of rules.
And each must make, ere life is flown,
A tumbling block or a stepping stone.'"

Bob Phillips

Abraham Lincoln

Started his life in a humble cabin reading by candlelight and going barefoot. He lost more elections than he won and at one point in his life suffered a complete nervous breakdown. Yet he rose from that to become one of the greatest leaders of all time. In fact he failed in business at the age of 21; was defeated in a legislative race at age 22; failed again in business at age 24; overcame the death of his sweetheart at age 26; had a nervous breakdown at age 27; lost a congressional race at age 34; lost a senatorial race at age 45; failed in an effort to become vice-president at age 47; lost a senatorial race at age 49; and was elected president of the United States at age 52.

Nelson Rockefeller

As a child Rockefeller was classified as "learning disabled." And that was just a fancy label for "dumb." But he overcame that learning problem to become a respected national leader.

Eleanor Roosevelt

Eleanor's father was fond of her, but her mother rejected the homely girl. At five years of age Eleanor swallowed a penny to attract attention and lived in fantasy as the mistress of her father's household for many years. Her mother finally separated from her alcoholic husband who died sometime later. While still pretty young, Eleanor was orphaned and willed to the custody of her grandmother. She had four young uncles living in the same household who could not really be managed by the widowed grandmother. One of these uncles was an alcoholic and would often lock himself in a room, another was asthmatic and the aunt on the paternal side was crippled. The grandmother resolved to be stricter with the children, so she dressed Eleanor oddly and refused to allow her to have playmates and did not send her to grade school. She was also put in a brace to keep her back straight.

This is the woman who said, "no one can hurt you without your consent." Of course she was not talking about physical but emotional hurt.

Albert Einstein

When Albert was in his senior year in secondary school he obtained a letter from his physician, stating that a nervous breakdown made it necessary for him to leave school for six months. He spoke late as a child and was not a good all-round student. He had a poor adjustment to school, had no friends and his teachers found him to be a problem. His father was ashamed of his son's lack of athletic ability. He had what was referred to as "mannerisms" part of which was making up his own religion and chanting hymns to himself. Indeed his parents regarded his as "different."

Thomas Edison

Thomas Edison had a large head at birth and so the doctors thought that he might have had "brain fever." Three of his siblings died before his birth. His mother did not agree with the relatives and neighbours that the child was probably abnormal. When he was sent to school the teacher diagnosed him as mentally ill. His mother was angry, withdrew him from school and decided to teach him herself.

Thomas Edison tried more than ten thousand different light bulbs before he made the one that worked. The average man would have quit after the first failure. That's why there are so many average men and only one Edison.

"It is my conviction that most people have within themselves great resources for solving their own problems and difficulties. With God's help and the use of the Bible, many problems will begin to resolve themselves, and for those that cannot be resolved, God will give the strength and grace to endure them.

God will give you the ability to make peace with pain."

Bob Phillips

Theodore Roosevelt

One of the greatest presidents of the USA. His enthusiasm and stamina seemed boundless. Nothing was an obstacle to Roosevelt. As the vice presidential candidate in 1900, he gave 673 speeches and travelled 20,000 miles while campaigning for President McKinley. And years after his presidency, while preparing to deliver a speech in Milwaukee, Roosevelt was shot in the chest by a would-be assassin. With a broken rib and a bullet in his chest, Roosevelt insisted on delivering his one-hour speech before allowing himself to be taken to the hospital. This was the same man who as a child was puny and very sickly. He had debilitating asthma, possessed very poor eyesight, and was painfully thin. His parents weren't sure he would survive.[12]

Champions don't become champions in the ring - they're merely recognised there. If you want to see where someone develops into a champion, look at his daily routine.
Theodore Roosevelt was a fan of boxing and one of his most famous quotes uses a boxing analogy:

'It is not the critic who counts, not the man who points out how the strong man stumbled, or where the doer of deeds could have done them better. The credit belongs to the man who is actually in the arena; whose face is marred by dust and sweat and blood; who strives valiantly; who errs and comes short again and again; who knows the great enthusiasms, the great devotions, and spends himself in a worthy cause; who, at best, knows in the end the triumph of high achievement; and who, at the worst, if he fails, at least fails while daring greatly, so that his place shall never be with those cold and timid souls who know neither victory nor defeat..'[13]

Beethoven composed some of the best music - and he was deaf. Some of the best poetry written on nature was written by Milton - and he was blind. One of the greatest world leaders was US President Franklin D. Roosevelt - and he served from a wheel chair.[14]

Failure doesn't mean you are a failure. It does mean you haven't succeeded yet.
Failure doesn't mean you have accomplished nothing. It does mean you have learned something.
Failure doesn't mean you have been a fool. It could mean you had a lot of faith.
Failure doesn't mean you have been disgraced. It does mean you're willing to try.
Failure doesn't mean you are inferior. It does mean you're not perfect.
Failure doesn't mean you've wasted your life. It does mean you have a reason to start afresh.
Failure doesn't mean you should give up. It does mean you should try harder.
Failure doesn't mean you'll never make it. It does mean it will take a little longer.
Failure doesn't mean God has abandoned you. It may mean God has a better idea.

When the night is past and the dawning of the new day is about to break with fresh hopes and dreams, then you will hear ---- the singing of the birds.
When the storm clouds break to drift away leaving bright patches of blue with golden shafts of sunlight on flower and leaf sparkling with fresh drops of diamond rain, then you will hear ---- the singing of the birds.
Yes, there are those times and places when the cold winter ends. Springtime returns. The dark night of the soul is dissolved in a happy daybreak. The storm is over. Then you will hear ---- the singing of the birds.
R.H.S.

It Can't Be Done?

People will always be willing to share their unsolicited opinions of what can't be done. Most of the men and women who have accomplished outstanding achievements were told that it couldn't be done. If they had believed that negative message many of the things we take for granted today that make life more enjoyable and convenient would not be in existence.

The 4-minute mile:

People had been trying to achieve it since the days of the ancient Greeks. In fact, folklore has it that the Greeks had lions chase the runners, thinking that would make them run faster. They also tried drinking tigers' milk. Nothing worked. So they decided that it was impossible. And for thousands of years everyone believed it. It was physiologically impossible for a human being to run a mile in four minutes. Our bone structure was all wrong. Wind resistance too great; inadequate lung power. There were a million reasons.

Then one man, one single human being, proved that the doctors, the trainers, the athletes, that the millions and millions before him who tried and failed, were all wrong. And miracle of miracles, the year after Roger Bannister broke the 4-minute mile, thirty-seven other runners broke the 4-minute mile, and the year after that three hundred runners broke the 4-minute mile.

"**Alexander Graham Bell**, that college professor had people laughed at him for his idiotic idea that the human voice could be carried along a wire. But today every time we pick up the telephone we salute the man who stayed on course, despite the laughter."[15]

Robert Fulton, the man who invented the steamship said of that experience, "never did a single encouraging remark, a bright hope, or a warm wish cross my path." And that's about what you expect when you try something new.

Consider the dirty thirteen-letter word "impossibility". When uttered aloud, this word is devastating in its effect. Thinking stops. Progress is halted. Doors slam shut. Research comes to a screeching halt. Further experimentation is torpedoed. Projects are abandoned. Dreams are discarded. The brightest and best of the creative brain cells nose-dive, clam up, hide out, cool down, and turn off in some dark subterranean corner of the mind. In this defensive manoeuvre, the brain shelters itself against the painful sting of insulting disappointments, brutal rejections and dashed hopes.

But let someone utter the magic words "it's possible." Those stirring words, with the siren appeal of a marshalling trumpet, penetrate into the subconscious tributaries of the mind, challenging and calling those proud powers to turn on and turn out new ideas! Buried dreams are resurrected. Sparks of fresh enthusiasm flicker, then burst into new flame. Tabled motions are brought back to the floor. Dusty files are reopened. Lights go on again in darkened laboratories. Telephones start ringing. Computer keyboards make clattering music. Budgets are revised and adopted. "Help wanted" signs are hung out. Factories are retooled and reopened. New products appear. New markets open. The recession has ended. A great new era of adventure, experimentation, expansion and prosperity is born. Alf Lohne

Tom was born without half of a right foot and only a stub of a right arm. As a boy, he wanted to engage in sports as the other boys did. He had a burning desire to play football, of all things. Because of his desire, his parents had an artificial foot made for him. It was made of wood. The wooden foot was encased in a special stubby football shoe. Hour after hour, day after day, he would try and keep on trying to make field goals from greater and greater distances.

He became so proficient that the New Orleans Saints hired him. Now, just offhand, what would you say a person's chance of playing professional football were, if he were born without half of a right foot and a withered arm? But the screams of 66,910 football fans would be heard throughout the United States when Tom Dempsey, with his crippled leg, kicked the longest field goal ever kicked in a professional football game... within the last two seconds of the game... to give the Saints a winning score of 19 to 17 over the Detroit Lions. "We were beaten by a miracle," said Detroit coach Joseph Schmidt. But it was not so much a miracle but perseverance.[16]

References: -

[1]Ringer, Robert (1990) **The 10 Habits of Highly Successful People** p.180 Advantage Quest Publications, Malaysia

[2]Khera, Shiv (1998) **You Can Win** p.111 Simon & Schuster Pte Ltd, Singapore

[3]Ringer, Robert (1990) **The 10 Habits of Highly Successful People** p.180

[4]Nightingale, Earl (1993) **The Essence of Success** p.338

[5]Ibid. p.37

[6]Nixon, Richard G. (1973) **The Lazy Man's Way To Riches** p.146 F.P. Publishing Co. Inc. Carson City, Nevada, USA

[7]Ibid. p.185

[8]Khera, Shiv (1998) **You Can Win** p.57

[9]Ringer, Robert (1990) **The 10 Habits of Highly Successful People** p.206

[10]Nixon, Richard G. (1973) **The Lazy Man's Way To Riches** p.120

[11]Ringer, Robert (1990) **The 10 Habits of Highly Successful People** p.228

[12]Maxwell, John C. (1998) **The 21 Irrefutable LAWS OF LEADERSHIP** P.30 Thomas Nelson, Inc. Nashville, Tennessee

[13]Ibid. p.29

[14]Khera, Shiv (1998) **You Can Win** p.112

[15]Nightingale, Earl (1993) **The Essence of Success** p.327

[16]Ibid. p.69

Section Six

USING THE HERE AND NOW

USING THE HERE AND NOW

Yesterday is a cancelled cheque; tomorrow is a promissory note; but today is cash in hand!

"Each day, well lived, makes every yesterday a dream of happiness and each tomorrow a vision of hope. Look well, therefore, to this one day, for it and it alone is life."
Earl Nightingale

"It is only when life is threatened that a conception of its value begins to dawn on the average person."
Earl Nightingale

The highest value that can be achieved by man is a deeper relationship with God.
George Barna

"Therefore God again set a certain day, calling it Today... as was said before: 'Today, if you hear his voice, harden not your hearts.' Hebrews 4:7 NIV

"And do this, understanding the present time. The hour is come for you to wake up from your slumber, because our salvation is nearer now than when we first believed." Romans 13:11

So, there are neon signs everywhere shaking us, warning us, jolting us, cajoling us to wake up, to get up, to stand up, to look up. From the most ancient wisdom book to the modern success authors we get the clarion call to use today, to use the here and the now. There is no other time. There is no better time. There is no easier time. Today is your day of salvation. Today is within your grasp. Use it! Use it! Extend that arm - take up that book. Flex that large leg muscle - begin that exercise programme. Get up from in front of that television. Wake up from that zombie-like living. Fill in that application form that has been gathering dust. Make that telephone call. Take up that pen and put it to the paper and begin the first few lines of that book. Move! This is Today - cash in hand. Soon it will be a cancelled cheque.

Look around you. If you have learned how to see - you will catch the movement of men and women who have discovered how to use Today. Look at their faces. Animated, joyful, relaxed, full of meaning and purpose. I'm obviously not speaking of the pinched, panicky, perturbed faces of those whose days control them and have them running down streets and cursing under their breaths at little old ladies who slow them down on the pavement. They too recognise the value of today. But they slept too late or they failed to plan the night before or the month before for that matter, so Today has caught them unawares and unprepared and they're attempting to make up time and woe to the person or animal that get in their way.

Stop Wallowing

Self-pity is an opiate.

Every minute spent wallowing over a past wrong or beating yourself for a past mistake is wasted time and wasted energy. If you feel so badly about it, if it makes you sick to think about it, then put your mental energy into seeing that it does not happen again. Use your brainpower and all your resources to show that you have learned from your mistake. When your subconscious attempt to take you over the same ground, reliving the mistake or the wrong over and over again, you do not need to give in and listen. Tell it to shut up and that you're moving on.

"Wallowing in guilt is not accepting responsibility. It is usually a way to avoid living in the here and now."[1] We have been given an effective way of handling guilt.

"If we confess our sins he (Jesus Christ) is faithful and just to forgive us our sins and to cleanse us from all unrighteousness. 1John 1:9 KJV.

"Come now and let us reason together says the Lord, though your sins are like scarlet, they shall be as white as snow; though they are red as crimson, they shall be as wool. Isaiah 1:18 NIV.

Micah 7:19 NIV. **"You will again have compassion on us; you will tread our sins underfoot and hurl all our iniquities into the depths of the sea.**

Of course we don't have to believe all the above; we can ignore this great offer; we can rubbish the greatest wisdom book on the planet and hug and nurse and cherish our guilt as if it's a treasured possession. But may I warn you, that will be like hugging a snake to our bosom. I've met people who refuse to forgive themselves. These are folk whose standards are higher than God's. What folly! God is willing to forgive them. But they refuse to forgive themselves because of their perfectionist attitude. I would rather go with the promises and commitment of a forgiving and gracious God and experience the wonderful freedom of having the burden of guilt lifted from my shoulders. Hey, if even you never believed, if even you doubt the very existence of God - what is there to lose?

Folk try mind-altering, destructive drugs, transcendental meditation, they soak up the advice of the positive thinking gurus of the modern world-- all in an effort to break free from the crippling, stifling, limiting prison of guilt, past mistakes and sometimes rank wickedness. I ask again, what then do you have to lose by taking hold of the three biblical references above and cashing in on the benefits they offer. I have led thousands to do so and they have marvelled at the simplicity and reality of a freedom that is impossible to adequately describe.

Then there are those who are wallowing and feel that they're justified. After all life has dealt them an unfair hand. And there are people who have been battered by life's blows - no denying that. There are people who were disadvantaged from the womb because their mothers decided to use drugs. There are others who were deposited into such dysfunctional homes and families that just to survive, to be alive today is a major accomplishment. Still, why have you gone through all that only to now succumb to crippling depression and destructive attitudes? The fact that you're alive today means that you're a survivor. You are not dead, are you? If warm blood is coursing through your veins- if you can read and understand these words- if you can hope and dream and use your imagination then you can stop feeling sorry for yourself and determine to be the best you can become.

Though even as I write these lines I recognise that there are some people out there who have been so beaten down by years of misfortune, accidents and bad habits -- some of you may have been so habituated in negative inner conversation that you're just not ready for this kind of talk. Some of you right now may be in the throes of depression -- although it can't be that bad or else you won't even be reading this book. But if you are; you really can't hear what I'm saying until you get some help to be functioning at "normal" level again. Without that help the gist of my writing may even irritate you. As one man said in one of my seminars "we are already not making it and you seem to be putting the blame on us." He used the wrong choice of word, which shows where he was at that present time. It has nothing to do with 'blame' the operative word is 'responsibility'. Am I putting the responsibility of your life squarely on your shoulders? You bet I am. Who do you want to take that responsibility -- Lady Luck, fate, circumstances, your parents, the government, the people around you, your husband or wife?

Don't Squander Time

Time is the stuff life is made of.

Man has conquered the world's highest mountains, the most treacherous white waters, and the coldest and most barren outback. He has obliterated certain disease scourges from the face of the earth (or so he thought). He has explored outer space and landed on the moon. But time remains unconquerable. "It cannot be expanded, accumulated, mortgaged, hastened or retarded. It is the one thing that is completely beyond man's control. And yet it is squandered as if there is no end to it."[2]

Even those more conscientious souls who take exception to the charge of squandering time are shocked once they begin to really monitor how they use time. They are puzzled at how much time slip through their fingers without them being able to account how it was spent. Where did the time go? This is a common question. Then there are those, whenever we speak to the time issue, who mistakenly believe that folk who are so conscious of the value of time can't really enjoy life. Their picture is that of people who do not know how to relax, to enjoy time. On the contrary, we are not speaking of an unhealthy preoccupation with time. Time for relaxation and recreation - time spent with people you love and people you help and people you can learn from are all factored in. So many come to the end of their life's journey and express regret about their use of time. One of the most common is "I regret not spending more time with the people who mean the most to me." We have never had one say "I regret not having spent more time at the office.

How many of us as children had our parents say to us: "There is a time for everything." How true. The times we were thrown this piece of ancient wisdom was usually when we were doing something that was not wrong in itself but was inappropriate or when we were carrying on with a particular activity beyond a reasonable time. They didn't make that up themselves. Here is where they got it.

"There is a time for everything, and a season for every activity under heaven.
A time to be born and a time to die, a time to plant and a time to uproot,
a time to kill and a time to heal, a time to tear down and a time to build,
a time to weep and a time to laugh, a time to mourn and a time to dance,
a time to scatter stones and a time to gather them,
a time to embrace and a time to refrain, a time to search and a time to give up,
a time to keep and a time to throw away, a time to tear and a time to mend,
a time to be silent and a time to speak, a time to love and a time to hate,
a time for war and a time for peace. Ecclesiastes 3:1-8 NIV.

Learn to enjoy Today

If a person cannot find meaning and value in his present, he will very likely be missing it in his future. Today is the future of five years ago. Are you enjoying it as much as you thought you would?

"If we find it difficult to enjoy the day in which we're living, we should remember that what we're waiting for will be made up of the same kind of days we're getting now."[3] We are being encouraged here to savour each day. Practice packing some enjoyment into each day instead of transferring or postponing genuine enjoyment for tomorrow or next year or the next. What features of today can you enjoy? One proven way of bringing enjoyment into an ordinarily flat day is to purposely set out to make somebody else's day. The happiness and satisfaction your thoughtfulness generates will spill over into your day like dew on a parched ground.

A second tip on how to enjoy today is to stop and spend a few minutes considering what simple natural beauty you can appreciate. It will surprise you no end, once you have gained some practice in this, how much joy, peace, satisfaction and contentment can be derived from the simplest things in life. Simple in the sense that they are within the everyday reach of everyone- rich and poor - but profound in the uncommon ability to extract beauty and value in things so common. I'm talking about flowers, birds, the animated conversation of lovers on a park bench, the valiant struggle of an ant to carry a load two or three times its body weight, experimenting with seeing how many strangers you can get to smile (exercise wisdom here, you can never go wrong with little old ladies).

"Most people place the greatest value on the cheapest things in life, while the greatest gift of all-- life itself -- goes unnoticed."[4] Millions slave all their lives without time to appreciate the smell of a rose in order to stock their houses full of society's modern gadgets and toys that they never get time to enjoy.

Parents hold down two jobs-- spend no time with their children in order to build or buy a dream home for the children. By the time they acquire the property the children are away at college and then they marry and go off on their own and leave the parents with a big, beautiful, empty and lonely house. By this time they barely hear from the children because they were so busy working hard they had no time to develop a meaningful relationship with the children. Many have slaved all their lives to become rich and then became the richest corpse in the cemetery. Remember life is what happens when you're busy planning for tomorrow. Does this mean that we should not spend time planning and working for tomorrow. No. But it does mean that we must watch our balance carefully. Human beings tend to be beings of extremes. True success calls for a balanced life. In this chapter I'm reminding you that you that while you do all the other necessary things do not neglect to enjoy today.

Watch the Time Spent on Tomorrow

"The future is not something that just happens; it is a reality that is created by those strong enough to exert control over their environment. The future is not a "done deal" waiting for a response. The future belongs to God and through Him to those who are driven to shape it."[5]

Tomorrow doesn't need your attention. It has the annoying habit of arriving ahead of schedule -- without your help. If you take care of today - your tomorrow will be taken care of. If you spend today wisely and wisely spend today you won't be bankrupt tomorrow. You may have to read the previous statement twice before you catch what I've really said.

Remember Today is Cash in Hand

"Few people, it seems, develop an awareness of daily living. In possession of the miracle of life, they pass through their days like automatons. In possession of the greatest gift on earth -- life itself -- they tell us by their actions that they don't even know they have it and haven't the slightest conception of its value, let alone an awareness that it is to be enjoyed to the fullest every day."[6]

I remember reading a story many years ago about a man who was sentenced to die for a crime he committed. On the morning of his execution he had to be transported just about a mile from the facility in which he was held to the place of execution. As he was driven in the high security police vehicle with just the tiniest of window to let in some light -- this man who knew that this was his last trip, his last ride, his last every thing, placed his face right up against that window and with a hunger never before experienced took in every single thing on his short journey to execution. Everything was significant. Every tree and flower. It seemed to him that every blade of grass was important. The faces of the few people he saw, the sky, a chance bird, a dog, a pigeon - things that he would ordinarily never have given a second glance, he soaked in and soaked up today, his last day on earth. He left for posterity a gem of a statement about those last few minutes of his life. He said, "it seemed to me that I lived more in those few minutes than I had lived all the other years of my life put together."

"Millions with the miracle of sight never really see the world about them until it's practically too late; millions with the inborn capacity to love, and to know the joy that loving brings, wait too late to express it."[7] Yes, I know, to express love is to make oneself vulnerable. But it's that very vulnerability that opens us up for the deepest and greatest enjoyment one can experience this side of heaven. So with your attempt to block out the possible pain you also block out the possible exquisite, soul-watering, life-giving experiences and emotions. I'm sorry I can't give credit for the following statement. I heard it since I was very young but never knew where it originated. " Better to have loved and lost than to have never loved."

Each day take some action calculated to move you closer to

your goals and toward fulfilment as a person; and recognise and be aware of the beauty around us.[8] That action need not be anything great or grand, but no matter how small if each day you take some action in relation to your goals you would be surprised at how it adds up.

"Getting older may be inevitable, but being old isn't." George Burns

As I said in my book "Take Charge of Your Health" I've met people in their early thirties who are already spent. They're drained, jaded, worn out, bushed, enfeebled and run-through. And yet there are people in their eighties whose eyes are still mischievous, feet still nimble, mind still alert, hands still steady and dreams still alive. I was sharing the benefits of taking hold of those principles that protect one's vital force.

Here in this book I'm emphasising the importance of the mental attitude in not giving up, not letting go to the passing of years and recognising that one can be old in years and still strong and vibrant in mind. Many relatively strong older folk take to the rocking chair not only physically but mentally as well. They put away their books, lock away their dreams, hang up their roaming clothes, refuses to buy any new trainers (walking or jogging shoes), give away their tools, scrap their unfinished projects. What happens as a result? Their brain cells take a nose-dive because of inactivity and lack of challenge. My advice is that you give away one thing -- that rocking chair!

The more certain you are about your purpose in life, the more focused you'll be on living in the present and the more enthusiastic you'll be in your day-to-day work.[9]

It's so with any journey - when you know exactly where you're going you're more enthusiastic. When you know where you're headed it's more difficult for people get you side-tracked with little petty side-paths and alleyways. If however you're not sure how your activity fits into the bigger picture or the journey then it's extremely easy to decide, well let me just watch this television programme, it looks interesting or let me just sleep a little longer for today, tomorrow I can do what I intended to do today.

You cannot master the principle of living in the here and now if you do not love what you're doing. If you do something only because you believe it will bring you riches then your days may not be happy days. Those who are fortunate to discover what they really enjoy doing have discovered the secret of LIVING every day. If you really love your work no one can predict what the rewards will be. Just think for a moment about Walt Disney trying to convince his bank manager that he could build a fortune based on a mouse? To the average person, a hamburger stand is just that, a hamburger stand, but to Ray Kroc it was a passion that grew into a multibillion-dollar hamburger-stand empire -- McDonald's.

Many people never discover until too late that striving is an end in itself. Dreaming and planning and sacrificing and stretching after your goals is part of living just as much as achieving. Many people discover with utter disbelief that the chase to accomplish or acquire was more exciting that the actual acquiring or achieving. When you become aware of this you do not postpone the enjoyment of life for when the goal is achieved -- you enjoy the journey.

Unless we identify what we value most and put our everyday lives in line with those values, we will plan and live reactively.[10] Living according to what each day throws up is a lousy way to live. Each day can throw up a lot of busy nonsense and empty trite. Is that how you want to spend your days? If not, then you need to line up your days in accordance with your values.

"The importance of tying values to goals and daily activities cannot be overstated."[11]

Make your everyday decisions based on which value is most important, not on the whim of the moment.[12] If we don't prioritise those values, we inevitably wind up with conflicting goals and daily activities and the constant need to make perplexing decisions.[13]

Important things are seldom urgent unless we make them so. So the things we plan to do and know we ought to get done are the things that keep getting put back for a later date. To read a good book does not feel as urgent as the ringing telephone. To study for that degree does not feel as urgent as that pressing invitation of a friend to attend a party. And so we keep servicing the urgent things that are not important at the detriment of the important things that are not urgent. Pay attention to this and you can revolutionise your life.

You cannot fight Natural Laws

To live successfully in the here and now you must understand and work with natural laws. You might as well work with them because they are immutable and consistent. "A natural law cannot be repealed." "Natural laws are fundamental patterns of nature and life that human experience and testing have shown to be valid. They describe things as they really are, as opposed to how we think they are or how we wish they were. Whether we agree with them or not, these laws ultimately govern our lives and operate independent of our awareness or wishes. By becoming aware of them and working with them, we can live safely and successfully. If we ignore them, we will fail and make ourselves and others miserable."[14] The only natural law some people seem to be aware of is the law of gravity. There are many others that are not as evident. For example there is the powerful natural law of giving ourselves in service to others and, in the process, finding that we have everything we really want and need. This is one of the great secrets of life.

It's this principle Jesus was teaching in his paradoxical statement: " For whosoever will save his life shall lose it: and whosoever will lose his life for my sake shall find it." Matthew 16:25 KJV. It takes a lot of self-discipline and faith in this natural law to actually practice it. It goes directly opposite to what our instincts push us to do. We are naturally selfish beings. Without a thought we will look out only for ourselves. If we do - if we attempt to 'save our life' that way we are doomed to a miserable existence. But the moment we begin to experiment with 'losing' our lives in service to others then we draw to ourselves an inner meaning and fulfilment that is difficult to put in words.

"Of all the beliefs we can have on our belief windows, this is among the most profound in our quest for inner peace."[15]

Clock or Compass

The clock has to do with schedules, appointments, deadlines, emergencies, goals, activities, calendars, programmes, speed and efficiency -- about how fast we can get it done. A pre-occupation with the clock tends to make a person hard and impersonal. Such a person usually gets an impressive amount accomplished but at the expense of relationships. He/she may be highly 'successful' but very unhappy and lonely. Nobody likes him/her. One needs to be effective with people rather than attempting to be efficient with them. The clock deals with efficiency.

"Time management essentially ignores the reality that most of our time is spent living and working with other people who cannot be controlled."[16]

The compass on the other hand has to do with vision, purpose, values, meaning, mission, direction, people, importance -- more a matter of what you do and why you do it, rather than how fast you get it done. This does not mean that time is not considered, but it does mean time-efficiency is not the driving force. Remember as we have been emphasising throughout this book that a truly successful person is a balanced person. Both the clock and the compass have an important role but the compass must be in the lead informing how we use the clock.

Importance and Urgency: Although we deal with both factors, one of them is the basic paradigm through which we view our time and our lives.[17] The average person is rushing head long through life, doing nothing important. Take a few minutes and watch little children. They are in perpetual motion, very busy, but accomplishing very little. Even more to the point - have you ever seen a dog chasing it's tail? He's really busy - building up speed, terribly focused, with a real sense of urgency, kicking up a lot of dust - but going no where.

Do not prioritise your schedule, schedule your priorities.

<u>We need to move beyond time management to life leadership.</u>

"Petty things become unimportant when people are impassioned about a purpose higher than self."[18] Remember one of the quotes with which we began this chapter: "The highest value that can be achieved by man is a deeper relationship with God." George Barna.

It's utterly ridiculous to see high and lofty themes go a-begging and men and women spending their whole lives caught up in who said what about whom and who has the bigger car and who is going out with whom and who dresses the best and who can come up with the most impressive status symbol.

Contrast all that with this: "Higher than the highest human thought can reach is God's ideal for his children." Ellen White

Yes. You can find a purpose higher than self to become impassioned about. You too can find your purpose and your unique contribution to society and to people around you. You too can lie in your bed just before daybreak quivering with excitement as you anticipate a day of making a difference, a day of opportunity, a day of exciting challenges. This is not a myth. This is not just a nice combination of words. There are people all around you who are living like this. The principles of how you can live this kind of life are what this book is all about. Don't put it aside as another book you have read. This is more like a manual for life. Keep it off the shelf, near at hand. Re-read relevant chapters or portions each day. You will be amazed how certain principles hit you as though you have not read them before because your mind is ready to receive them at this moment and not before. Success is within your grasp. Take hold of it with your entire being.

References: -

[1]Nixon, Richard G. (1973) **The Lazy Man's Way To Riches** p.188
[2]Nightingale, Earl (1993) **The Essence of Success** p.433
[3]Ibid. p.434
[4]Ibid. p.436
[5]Barna, George (1992) **The Power of Vision** p.48
[6]Nightingale, Earl (1993) **The Essence of Success** p.436
[7]Ibid. p.435
[8]Ibid. p. 438
[9]Ringer, Robert (1990) **The 10 Habits of Highly Successful People** p.94
[10]Smith, Hyrum W. (1995) **The 10 Naural Laws of Successful Time & Life Management** p.75
[11]Ibid. p.74
[12]Ibid. p.71
[13]Smith, Hyrum W. (1995) **The 10 Natural Laws of Successful Time & Life Mangement** p.68
[14]Ibid. p.12
[15]Ibid. p.212
[16]Covey, Stephen R. (1994) **First Things First** p.26
[17]Ibid. p.32
[18]Ibid. p.106

HEALTH COURSE OFFER

Total Health Seminars, the publisher of this book offers a valuable, informative, interesting Health Course with an impressive Certificate on completion. The course was designed and written by Hamilton Williams, the author of this book.

26 Lessons done in the comfort of your Home

1. What is Health?
2. Healthy Eating
3. Equilibrium
4. Water and Your Health
5. Coffee Break Can Break You
6. Exercise and Your Health
7. The Benefits of Exercise
8. Obesity - the Incorrect Solution
9. Obesity - the Correct Solution
10. Avoiding Cancer
11. Help for Headaches
12. How to Have Younger Skin
13. Stroke! How to Avoid a Killer
14. Is Your Heart in shape?
15. Understanding Stress
16. Managing Stress
17. Water Treatments
18. Coping with Crisis
19. Health Secrets of the Bible
20. Cleaning our Your Arteries
21. Mind Over Matter
22. Diabetes - Prevention
23. Eat for Health
24. Cleansing the Colon
25. Secrets of the Longest Living People
26. How Much Do You Remember?

Recommended book to accompany course: **Take Charge of Your Health by**
Hamilton J. Williams

Cost of Course: £35 - includes marking of lessons, postage and certificate.

Telephone: 07956 546338 E-mail: Hamwill@aol.com

JOIN THE ELITE - HAVE A LIFE COACH

The concept of a life coach is better known among the top-notch elite business people. Not because only these people need life coaches, but because it's usually financially beyond the reach of corporate business people. This unique offer is bringing it within your reach.

A life coach is someone who assists you in setting your life goals and charting a course for meeting those goals. He contacts you and communicates by telephone, e-mail or face to face meetings to monitor your progress and keep you motivated and moving towards those life goals that you have set.

He assists you in discovering why you may not be achieving your goals and challenges you to get back on track when personal tragedy or emotional upheaval has derailed you.

Just like an athletic coach assists the athlete in achieving his greatest potential, so a life coach assists the individual in achieving his life goals and becoming him/her best self.

If you have been starting and abandoning health practices or constantly floundering in other areas of your life and you suspect that you could achieve much more if you become focused or remain motivated then please call to find out more about Life Coaching: